ENDLESS

ENDLESS

KATE BRIAN

HYPERION

LOS ANGELES • NEW YORK

alloyentertainment
Produced by Alloy Entertainment
1700 Broadway, New York, NY 10019

First Edition
1 3 5 7 9 10 8 6 4 2
V475-5664-5-14121
Printed in the United States of America

This book is set in Janson Text
Designed by Liz Dresner

Library of Congress Cataloging-in-Publication Data
Brian, Kate.
  Endless / Kate Brian.—First edition.
    pages cm—(Shadowlands)
  Summary: When Rory Miller learns that her love, Tristan Parrish, has been seeking a second chance at life on Earth by sending good souls to the Shadowlands, including her friend Aaron, her father, and her sister Darcy, she will do anything to save them, even if that means going to hell and back.
  ISBN 978-1-4231-6485-2 (hardback) —ISBN 1-4231-6485-7
[1. Dead—Fiction. 2. Future life—Fiction. 3. Sisters—Fiction. 4. Single-parent families—Fiction. 5. Islands—Fiction. 6. South Carolina—Fiction. 7. Horror stories.] I. Title.
  PZ7.B75875End 2014
  [Fic]—dc23   2014010212

Reinforced binding

Visit www.hyperionteens.com

SUSTAINABLE FORESTRY INITIATIVE Certified Sourcing
www.sfiprogram.org
SFI-00993

THIS LABEL APPLIES TO TEXT STOCK

For my family, with endless love

THE BELL TOLLS

"Rory, stop!"

I tried to freeze, but the muddy, rocky path beneath my left foot began to slip, crumbling into the deep roadside river below. Rain pounded on my useless vinyl hood as I grasped at the air with cold, wet fingers. I was finally able to grab the slippery fabric of Joaquin Marquez's sleeve, and he hoisted me back up onto solid ground, my heart pounding in my throat at a maddening rate. The muddy pathway we were traversing had been, until recently, wide enough for at least one car, if not two, to navigate safely. But now it was half its former width and eroding by the moment.

1

The rain had been nonstop since Saturday night. Now it was Wednesday, and half the island of Juniper Landing seemed to have turned to mush. The sand on the beaches had taken on the consistency of oatmeal in spots, and the grasses and reeds and flowers had been flattened to the ground, beaten into submission by the relentless weather.

"Are you okay?" Joaquin asked.

I nodded, clutching both his elbows for stability. His brown eyes were shaded by the brim of his own hood, and a few days' worth of dark stubble covered his sharp cheekbones and chin. This had become a habit of Joaquin's lately—saving me from serious injury. I wasn't sure how I felt about the fact that the boy my sister used to hook up with was now my protector, but I was grateful to have someone by my side. And it clearly wasn't going to be the boy *I* used to hook up with. He was no longer around.

Which was why we were out here in the first place—looking for Tristan Parrish. The guy I had been falling in love with, until a few days ago. The guy who had betrayed us all. According to Joaquin, there was a cave beneath the bridge where Tristan used to go to for his "big thinks"—the days he just wanted some space away from the other Lifers. Unfortunately, it was located in a part of the island Joaquin had always avoided unless he was ushering a visitor to the bridge, so we weren't entirely clear on where we were going.

That, plus the relentless rain, didn't make our mission any easier.

"Is this ever going to stop?" I asked.

As if in answer, a bolt of lightning cracked overhead and the whole world trembled with the accompanying thunder. Over Joaquin's shoulder I saw a shadow illuminated by the flash—someone standing on a rock ledge not fifty yards away, raincoat billowing in the wind. My fingernails dug into Joaquin's arm.

"Is that . . . ?"

Joaquin turned, but just like that, there was no one there. One blink, and the shadow had disappeared. The storm was playing tricks on my mind.

"What?" Joaquin asked.

"Nothing. Forget it." I didn't want to admit I was seeing things. "I just can't handle much more of this."

"Relax. Take a breather," Joaquin said. "Let me figure out where the hell we are."

As he moved off to peer into the grayness surrounding us, I tried to shake the jittery feeling that shadow had left behind and looked north toward the bridge. It was so encased in fog that I could see nothing but the pointless warning lights throbbing at the top of its four spires. The bridge had become—to me, anyway—the symbol of everything that was wrong on this island. Juniper Landing was an in-between—a place where souls came to reside between death and the afterlife, a place where they were given a chance to resolve any issues that might have plagued them during their lifetimes before moving on. Joaquin and I were both Lifers, a group of souls charged with helping others find their resolutions and ushering them to their final destinations. The bridge was the means of transport. When a soul was ready to go, we would take the person to the bridge and hand him or her a coin. As soon as he or she touched the coin, it just sort of knew whether that soul was destined for the Light or the Shadowlands, based on how good or evil the person had been in life. We would then usher that person across the bridge, where a portal would open, taking him or her to the proper place. This was a system that had been in place since the dawn of time and had always worked perfectly, maintaining the balance of the universe.

Until now. Recently the whole thing had gone haywire, with devastating consequences. We were pretty sure that the coins were somehow to blame, since Tristan had been hiding a whole bag of them—more than any Lifer had ever seen in one place at one time—and had fled the second the rest of us discovered his stash. We weren't clear on what exactly was wrong with the coins, how they had been tampered with, or where Tristan had even gotten them. All we knew was that last week, a few souls who were undeniably good had wound up in the Shadowlands. Souls like my friend Aaron and Joaquin's charge Jennifer. Souls like my father. They were good people, damned to hell, and soon after they had left, we caught Tristan with the coins.

Something lodged in my throat at the mere thought of my dad in the Shadowlands—alone, terrified, possibly tortured—and for a second, I couldn't breathe.

"I think it's this way," Joaquin said, nodding toward the bridge. "Let's keep moving."

I let him lead the way, allowing myself one glance back over my shoulder at the spot where the shadow had been. The outcropping was deserted. I breathed in and out deliberately, trying to calm the frantic beating of my heart. As we moved closer to the bridge, I could just make out two figures clad in black rain gear, their nebulous forms like dark ghosts, moving in and out of my waterlogged vision. Ever since we'd discovered the tainted coins, the Lifers had been taking turns guarding the bridge, to insure no one could cross over. I had no idea who was scheduled to be there now, and from this distance through the rain, I couldn't make out their faces. For some reason, their dark presence felt ominous instead of comforting.

It's going to be okay, I told myself. *You're going to fix this. You just have to find Tristan and Nadia and make them tell you how to fix it.*

Tristan. The image of him and his smiling, duplicitous face twisted my stomach into knots. I had believed in him. I had trusted him more than anyone. I had loved him. And he'd betrayed me. I had been suspected of ushering good souls to the Shadowlands, and then it was finally revealed that Tristan was the villain. Tristan, who had told me that the rules of this place couldn't be broken. That I had to trust in the system. That everything would be fine.

He'd said those things to me. He'd kissed me. He'd made me feel safe. And then he'd ushered my father straight to hell.

Joaquin and I turned up an even scrawnier, more circuitous path, leading toward the drop-off into the ocean, toward the very foot of the bridge. As a cold rivulet of water found its way under my collar and down my back, I couldn't help wondering, for the millionth time, *Why?* Why had Tristan done this to Aaron, to Jennifer, to my dad . . . to all of us? What did he stand to gain? And, most selfishly, why had he done this to me? Why suck me in and make me care? Why make me believe in him and everything this place was about, only to turn around and betray me and destroy his home?

Joaquin looked back at me and held out a hand. I grasped his fingers, half expecting them to slip away from me, but his grip was surprisingly solid. A few weeks ago I never would have believed that I would one day willingly hold Joaquin's hand. When I first met him, I had hated him. He was *that* guy. That guy who knew how hot he was and used that fact to toy with the heart of any girl who showed an interest in him. In this case, that girl had been my sister, Darcy.

But the more I got to know Joaquin, the more I respected him. He truly cared about his charges, about his friends, and about this place. And when things had started to go sideways, he'd basically become my personal bodyguard. And over the past few days, since we'd found out Tristan was the big bad around here, we bonded even more. No one wanted to find Tristan more than we did. Joaquin had been his best friend. I'd been Tristan's girlfriend. (Would-be-ex-girlfriend the second I saw him again.) We *needed* to find him. We needed to ask him that one burning question: *Why?*

It was what kept us going—the hope that we would one day get the answers we were looking for: why he had done what he'd done, how he could betray everyone he claimed to care about, and, most important, how to free my dad and Aaron and Jennifer and those other poor souls. What I didn't know was what we were going to do with Tristan and Nadia—another Lifer who'd disappeared with Tristan—once we'd found them. My brain didn't even want to go there.

"I think it's down there," Joaquin said, squinting downward, tiny droplets clinging to the ends of his thick eyelashes. "I noticed the pathway the other day. It's kind of like a series of steps cut into the rock."

I didn't see anything, but I shrugged. "You lead the way."

Together we started slowly and carefully down the side of the drop-off. My foot slipped on the very first step, and Joaquin's grip on me tightened. We both froze.

"You good?" Joaquin asked.

I nodded mutely.

"Okay. Stay behind me and be careful."

He didn't have to ask me twice.

We descended the steep stairway in silence, and I focused on the sound of my own breathing, the plop of raindrops on my hood, the crashing of the waves far below, and the cautious positioning of my feet. But I couldn't help thinking of the look on Tristan's face the day we'd found the bag of tainted coins in his room. The realization in his gorgeous blue eyes that he'd been caught.

I wasn't stupid. I knew what I'd seen. Tristan was guilty. I just wished my heart would catch up with my brain and start believing it.

After what seemed like a lifetime, Joaquin jumped the last couple of feet to a foot-wide stretch of broken shells and sand that ran along the foot of the rocks. I leaped down after him, lifted my head, and saw it—the wide-open mouth of a cave.

"Score," Joaquin said.

Every inch of my skin flushed with heat, making me itch beneath my vinyl jacket. Tristan was in there. Maybe with Nadia, maybe not. Either way, we were about to get some answers.

And I was going to see him again.

I narrowed my eyes and clenched my teeth. Stupid heart.

Through the fog and the rain, I noticed a pile of something white and gray near the mouth of the cave. As we edged closer, I saw the blood. The glassy eyes, the twisted necks, the torn and shredded feathers. Dead seagulls. Dozens of them. Broken, deformed, and staring. Flies buzzed around their misshapen heads, and as I watched, one of them landed hungrily on the dome of a wide, glassy eye. Within seconds a swarm of them had engulfed the seagull's skull.

Then the wind shifted and the stench hit me like a brick in the face. I turned my nose away and covered my mouth with a hand.

"Just keep walking," Joaquin said, quickening his steps.

We passed by the carcasses and into the coverage of the cave. The sand near the opening was thick and sloppy, and my sneakers let out a sucking sound every time I lifted a foot. I nudged my hood from my head, relieved to be out of the rain even as my breath quickened. I could already smell the pungent scent of a recent fire.

Joaquin and I locked eyes. He tugged his flashlight from his jacket pocket but didn't turn it on, and he raised one finger to his mouth. I nodded. Moving in sync, we tiptoed forward. Joaquin paused for a moment at a corner and peeked around it. He visibly relaxed and flicked on his light.

"They're not here."

Deflated, I stepped out into an open area of the cave, the ceiling only five inches from the crown of my head. It was a wide space, and as Joaquin flashed his light to and fro, something caught my eye against the far wall.

"There!"

I grabbed his shoulder and pointed. Joaquin swung the beam back around, and it caught on something—a blue-and-white blanket. We raced for it. I got there first and dropped to my knees. The sand in this part of the cave was cold but dry. I whipped the blanket aside and stopped breathing. Underneath it was a crowbar, a first aid kit, and a hammer, with a few balled-up, bloody bandages tossed alongside. There were also two small piles of folded clothes—his and hers—several granola bars still in their wrappers, and three full bottles of water.

"So they were here," I whispered, irritated at the flash of jealousy I felt at the sight of Tristan's clothes folded next to Nadia's in such a cozy-couple way. Outside, thunder rumbled, but it was muted by the miles of rock over our heads.

"What were they doing with a crowbar?" Joaquin asked, crouching. He tentatively picked up one of the bandages by the clean end. "And whose blood is this?"

I shivered. "I don't want to know."

Joaquin dropped the scrap back into the sand and stood up, dusting off his hands. He was tense. I grabbed the light and flashed it along the floor, finding the remnants of their fire. It was still smoldering. Joaquin cursed under his breath.

"We just missed them," he said. "They were right here."

"Well, this is good, right? They can't have gotten far." I shoved myself up, the adrenaline pumping. "We can track them."

"How?" Joaquin demanded, whirling on me. "It's not like they're leaving footprints out there! The rain'll make sure of that!"

"You don't have to yell at me," I shot back. "What do you want to do? Just stand here? Let them get away?"

I turned toward the mouth of the cave, and Joaquin followed, his flashlight beam dancing ahead of us.

"You're about to go out on a wild-goose chase," Joaquin muttered. "And it's going to start getting dark."

"This whole thing is a wild-goose chase!" I cried, throwing my arms wide. "But this is the best lead we've had in three days. We can't just go home."

Joaquin grabbed my arm, turning me roughly toward him as I tried to lift my hood.

"But how are you even going to—"

His question was cut off by the distant clanging of a bell. It sounded like one of those old church bells they used to ring at the chapel near my house in Princeton whenever someone got married. Except this wasn't a merry, celebratory song. It was a frantic, uneven plea. Joaquin went white.

"What is that?" I asked.

"The bell." He turned away, facing south toward town, which wasn't visible from the foot of this cliff.

"Yes, I know it's a bell," I said. "What does it mean?"

"It means there's an emergency." He scrambled back toward the rocky stairway, past the pile of seagull carcasses, and over the broken shells.

"What kind of emergency?" I asked, sliding and slipping after him.

He paused with one foot on the third step, stretching his long legs as far as they would go, and looked back over his shoulder. I'd never seen him so terrified.

"I don't know," he said. "That bell hasn't been rung since Jessica got those innocent people damned to the Shadowlands, Rory. It hasn't been rung in a hundred years."

DESTRUCTION

The rain stung my face as we sprinted toward town, my feet slipping on fallen leaves, my lungs burning from the effort. My nostrils prickled with the ominous scent of dank, billowing smoke. Over the constant thrum of the rain and whooshing of the wind, I caught an errant scream, echoed by a dozen more. Joaquin's eyes were wild as they met mine, and we ran even harder.

When we finally arrived at the point overlooking the town square and the docks below, I was so stunned by what I saw I almost skidded right over the rocky ledge. Somehow

I managed to stop myself in time and doubled over next to Joaquin, heaving for breath.

The ferry that had always brought new souls to Juniper Landing was on fire and sinking—fast. The entire back of the vessel had gone up in flames. The air was torn with shouts and screams, and I could see several prone figures lined up on the bay's meager shore. Dozens of others clung to jagged shards of wood in the choppy, roiling surf or desperately swam for land, while Lifers dove in from the docks to help.

"Holy shit," Joaquin said between gasps.

We sprinted down the hill, skidding by the library and along the west side of town toward the docks. The air here was thick with smoke. We passed a few dazed Lifers in the shopping district, each of them frozen, their eyes shot through with confusion and fear as they watched the disaster unfold before them. It was an eerie sort of stillness to pass through before reaching the chaos of the docks. The long walkway was flanked on either side by slick, steep outcroppings of rocks. Bodies of the injured were laid out on the shore, while the more mobile survivors made their way to the rocky slope or up the stairs to the docks. Everywhere I looked, my friends and fellow Lifers were helping however they could.

Darcy's current boyfriend, Fisher Morton, tossed a person onto his broad shoulders and carried him to the sand before turning right back around and swimming out again. Bea McHenry was towing three people toward shore as they clung to a large chunk of the boat's prow. Farther down the dock, Krista Parrish and Lauren Caldwell helped patch up scrapes and bruises and burns, while a few strangers wandered aimlessly, shouting names or pleading for help. I yanked off my jacket and ran for the water. Joaquin was right behind me.

"Stop right there."

The sound of the mayor's commanding voice froze me in my tracks. I turned to find her standing on the rocks near the water's edge beneath a huge black umbrella, her blond hair slicked back in a low bun, her black raincoat cinched at the waist. Her ice-blue eyes flicked over me.

"They need help!" I shouted.

"Let them handle it," she said, nodding at the swimmers, who included my sister. "We need more hands out here cataloging the injuries."

Cataloging the injuries? Who the hell talked like that? But as I looked around at the wounded visitors huddled or lying on the slim stretch of sand, I saw that she was right. These people couldn't die, of course, but we had to find the ones in critical pain and separate them from those with simple bumps and bruises.

"Joaquin! Rory! I need some help over here."

Krista—Tristan's "sister" in the world of Juniper Landing, and as of the last few weeks, my friend—waved us down. She stood next to a man whose arm hung limply, the bone jutting at an unnatural angle. She had on a white raincoat over her jeans, but her blond hair was lifeless, and her skin was as pale as ice. Joaquin raced to her side just as Kevin Calandro and Officer Dorn sped up on a flatbed truck loaded with boxes, stopping in the parking lot at the top of the hill.

"We have the supplies!" Kevin shouted, swinging down from the cab. His normally shaggy black hair was slicked back from his face, and he wore a black tank top that exposed the colorful tattoo of flames that danced over his arm. His pointy chin rose in determination as he yanked open the back of the truck.

"Get us a splint!" Joaquin shouted at me. "And a sling!"

I ran to Kevin and helped him unload, tearing boxes open at random. The containers were full of first aid supplies, from ointments and creams to bandages, scissors, and stitching kits. In the third crate I found a dozen blue-and-white slings and flat plastic splints. I grabbed a set and stood.

"Here. You'll need this." Kevin tossed me a roll of medical tape, which I caught in my free hand.

"Thanks," I said, then sprinted for Joaquin and Krista,

checking the chaos for Darcy along the way. Where was she? Was she okay?

"I need help. I need help," a mocking voice passing very close behind me mimicked the victims.

My shoulder muscles coiled and my blood turned cold as Ray Wagner, one of my charges, stomped by in his dirty brown coat, his wispy hair sticking up on one side, even in the relentless rain. I ignored him and jumped down to the beach, but he leaned into the dock's railing above my head and laughed, exposing his yellow teeth and a tongue that had been blackened by chewing tobacco. With the rain running freely down his face, he spat in the sand and smiled, as if settling in to watch a ball game.

"What should I do?" I asked Joaquin, who was holding a man's arm as gently as possible. The man's face was purple with pain, and the wrinkles on his forehead deepened whenever he moved. Krista had stepped back, watching the proceedings with wide blue eyes. She looked as if she was hanging on by a thread.

"Put the sling over his head, gently. And hand me the splint," Joaquin ordered.

"You'll be okay," I told the man, slipping the white band over his head. "Don't worry. We've got you."

"Don't worry. Don't worry. Blah, blah, blah," Ray mocked me, tilting his head from side to side.

I shot him a look of death, but he simply laughed.

Ray Wagner had slaughtered four people in a one-night killing spree in Richmond, Virginia, before getting shot dead in a convenience store parking lot while trying to take out his fifth victim. Normally, I would have done my best to usher him as soon as possible, but since things were all out of whack and the no-ushering policy was in place, he was still here. As were a few other unsavory characters my friends had yet to usher. Lauren had been charged with a white-collar criminal named Piper Molloy, who had swindled dozens of families out of their life savings and rendered them homeless. Bea had a woman who had stepped off the ferry two days ago looking as if she'd come right out of the Stone Age with her scraggly hair, dirty fingernails, and gnarly teeth. Her name was Tess Crowe and she'd murdered her own parents, brother, and sister before being relegated to an insane asylum. Bea currently had her locked up in the attic of the home she shared with two older Lifers. Supposedly Tess kept her hosts up at night screeching and trying to claw her way out.

There had been some talk of locking up the visitors meant for the Shadowlands in the jail beneath the police station, but it was comprised of only two tiny cells and wasn't equipped to hold them all, so for now, we were each tasked with babysitting them as best we could—making sure they didn't cause any trouble. Ray was the only one, however, whose sadistic heart had been drawn to today's devastation. Lucky me.

"Oh god! That hurts!" the man cried out as Joaquin taped his arm to the splint.

"Almost done," I said as Joaquin used his teeth to rip the tape.

Once he'd secured the arm with four tight circles of tape, we gently maneuvered it into the sling. Then I carefully helped the man sit down on one of the dock's pylons.

"Thank you," he said, slumping slightly.

"Just hang out here while we figure out where to take you," Joaquin said.

"Thanks, you guys," Krista said, stepping between us with her knees wobbling. "I had no idea what to do."

"It's okay," Joaquin said. "The question is: what next?"

We scanned the water and the beach. Nearby a woman was sobbing next to her bleeding husband. A man staggered past us and collapsed onto the sand, his chest heaving for breath. Joaquin had nailed it. Where were we supposed to start? Then I saw a flash out of the corner of my eye: my sister's dark hair as she ran for the water. She was wearing nothing but shorts and a tank top and was soaked to the bone. Clearly this was not her first time diving into the bay.

"Darcy!" I shouted. But she didn't hear me. She plunged

beneath the choppy waves, reemerged, and swam straight for a little girl whose arms flailed as she went under, choking. My hands flew up to cover my mouth as Darcy plunged after her. I watched the whitecaps where they'd disappeared, scanning for any sign of them. But I could only see the spot where my sister and the girl had gone under.

Where are they? I thought, clenching my jaw.

"There!" Joaquin shouted, startling me. He pointed a good ten feet to the left of where I'd been looking, and there was Darcy, gamely swimming for shore with one arm locked around the little girl's chest. "She's okay." He gave my shoulder a quick squeeze. "They're both fine."

"Who's *that*?" Krista asked.

A sinewy, strong guy about our age was swimming toward the shore, holding a middle-aged woman tight around her chest, her chin tilted up toward the sky so she could breathe. He placed her on the shore, then raced right back out to the ferry to grab a man who still clung to the doomed ship's guardrail. Quickly, he pried the panicked man's fingers from the railing and brought him back to safety, then went out again, cutting through the water like it was nothing to him.

"Where did he come from?" I asked.

"I have no idea," Joaquin said.

Darcy had just gotten back to the shore and pulled the

little girl to safety. I ran to her side, slipping over the rocks until I reached the sand.

"Darcy! Are you guys okay?" I asked, dropping to my knees next to her.

Darcy flung her wet dark hair over her shoulder. She was winded but otherwise seemed fine. The girl, however, was wailing.

"She may have broken her leg, and look at her skin. She's so pale. I think we should get her to the hospital. Where the hell are the EMTs, already? Or the Coast Guard?"

I swallowed hard. Darcy had no clue about the realities of where we were. As far as she knew, we were still alive, enrolled in the witness protection program thanks to Steven Nell, and about to get a call any day saying he'd been apprehended and we could return to Princeton, to our home and our friends. She didn't know that a place like Juniper Landing didn't need any personnel dedicated to saving lives, because no one here had a life to save.

"Um . . . maybe the weather is screwing things up?"

"Well, we have to get her to a hospital," Darcy insisted.

Joaquin, who was now tending to a woman nearby, glanced over at me. "We don't exactly have a hospital," he said reluctantly.

"No hospital?" We looked up to find Super Swimmer Boy hovering over us, heaving for breath, his jet-black hair dripping water down his square cheekbones. "What do you mean, there's no hospital?"

His skin was a healthy tan, and he had one blue eye and one brown eye. The whole package was so handsome and startling I found myself staring. Darcy rose to her feet next to me, as speechless and transfixed as me.

"Yes, they're different colors. No, I don't know how or why," he stated, not amused, but not angry, either. Then he focused on Joaquin. "What do you do, then? Go to one on the mainland?"

"How would we even get everyone there without the ferry?" Darcy said, gesturing around wildly.

Now it was Joaquin's turn to be stumped. "Um . . . we . . . "

The seconds ticked by slowly. Strangers began to gather, having overheard our conversation, the injured cradling their arms or holding torn scraps of fabric against wounds. Everyone seemed to wait on whatever it was Joaquin would say next.

"Take them to the clinic."

An unpleasant shiver raced down my spine. I looked up at the plank walkway leading to the town and saw Mayor Parrish looking down at the rest of us.

"The clinic?" I asked.

"Of course," she said, rolling her eyes. "The clinic."

Then she gestured oh-so-elegantly up at the bluff, where her gorgeous, sprawling colonial mansion sat overlooking the town.

"Come now, everyone," she said loudly. "Let's help those who can't help themselves. Once we're settled inside and out of this rain, we can assess the situation."

For a long moment, no one moved. Not that anyone could have blamed us. This was not normal procedure for a disaster, following the snappish mayor up the hill with no EMTs or nurses, no ambulances, no nothing.

But this was Juniper Landing, and I'd long since learned that nothing around here was normal procedure. It wouldn't be long before everyone else here figured it out as well.

UNEXPECTED

People scream and cry and beg around me, but for the moment, I am still. I watch the prow of the ferry slowly sink beneath the surface of the water, and then it is gone. Completely gone. This, I was not expecting. Without the ferry, there will be no new souls. The pickings will begin to grow slim, and I haven't met my goal yet. I haven't completed my assignment. I still need five more.

But it's okay. I'll just have to focus. I have to make sure that only the good are taken, not the bad. Taking the bad is fine, but, for me, a waste of time. I must fulfill my destiny before they find me, before they figure me out.

I turn away as a hand reaches out to me, and watch Rory Miller help some poor, bloodied woman up the steps to a waiting truck. Soon, it will be up to her. She just doesn't know it yet.

THE CLINIC

"So, what's your name?"

Super Swimmer Boy stared straight ahead as he walked, the little girl Darcy had saved clinging to him with her tiny arms around his neck. Darcy had gone ahead with Krista to get into some dry clothes. The little girl's blond hair hung in wet hanks down her back, and she sniffled continuously, her cheek resting on his shoulder. The elderly-but-spry woman I was helping held fast to my waist, each step we took over the wind-flattened grass slow but steady. She had a deep gash on her forehead near her hairline and was holding a wad of gauze to it with her free hand, but she seemed otherwise unharmed. Out on the bay, the water slowly swallowed the bow of the ferry. I couldn't believe it was gone.

"Liam," he said. His tone was somehow mournful as he gazed steadily ahead. "Liam Murtry."

"I'm Rory Thayer," I offered.

He glanced at me so briefly I wasn't sure I hadn't imagined it. "Nice to meet you."

"And I'm Myra Schwartz," my patient offered, touching her chest. Droplets of rain dotted the lenses of her red-framed glasses. "What's your name, honey?" she asked, tilting her head to better see the little girl, her smile kind.

"I'm not supposed to talk to strangers," the girl said in a meek voice that broke my heart.

Myra nodded. "Good girl." Then she winked at me as if to say, *We're in this together.* I smiled gratefully in return.

"Behind you, Rory!" someone shouted.

Liam reached out and tugged me and Myra toward him as Kevin and Fisher passed, toting an old-school stretcher of canvas and wood between them. On it, a heavyset man in a suit groaned, his arm flung over his head to ward off the rain. They raced by as Liam and I watched, his strong fingers still gripping my biceps. I looked down at his hand and waited.

"Sorry," he said, recovering himself. He released me and grimaced. "It's just . . . this is some scene."

I took a breath, really looking around me for the first time since we'd started for the mayor's house. Officer Dorn had set up a makeshift command post near the bottom of the hill, handing out the stretchers he and Kevin had retrieved from the police station's basement along with the other supplies. There were only a few, so he was busy assessing injuries to decide who needed one and who didn't, his buzz-cut blond hair covered by the hood of a huge army-green poncho. Pete Sweeney and Cori Morrison passed by, supporting a limping man between them. Pete was stooping to try to even out the marked height difference between him and Cori. Bea and Ursula, the older Lifer whom Joaquin shared a home with as pseudo grandmother and grandson, carried a woman on a stretcher whose skin looked waxy and green. There were new arrivals everywhere, wincing, groaning, crying—doing the best they could to make it up the steep hill as Lifers darted around trying to help. The girl in Liam's arms shifted her head to look at me.

"Where's my mom?"

Liam's eyes met mine. "We'll find her," he assured her, running his hand down the back of her head. "Don't worry. We'll find her."

My throat constricted as we kept moving, Myra's fingers gripping my jacket. I knew in my heart that we probably wouldn't find her mother. Unless the girl had died along with her mom in an accident of some kind, she was here alone. Most children stayed on Juniper Landing for approximately five seconds before they were ushered to the Light, too young to have unresolved issues or to have done anything in life that would mark them for the Shadowlands. But since we'd stopped ushering people, the few kids who had shown up here these last, agonizing days were still here. One adorable boy named Oliver had wept nonstop for his parents upon arrival, until the mayor had taken him aside and worked her magic on his mind, basically making him forget he'd ever had parents. He'd jumped up and run off to the other brainwashed kids to start a game of tag. It was the first time I understood the real benefit of her powers.

"You were pretty impressive out there," I told Liam, trying to change the subject.

He lifted his shoulders as best he could. "I'm a lifeguard. It's what I do."

We were making our way up the path to the mayor's front door, the pavement lined with dead brown marigolds and piles of wet, withered leaves—things we wouldn't have seen in Juniper Landing when we first arrived here, when even the plants could never die. A sort of traffic jam had occurred near the front of the house, and people stood on their toes, angling for a look at the front of the line. Liam's charge started to whimper.

"This looks like it's going to take a while," Myra stated, her brown eyes full of concern as she looked at the girl.

"Come with me," I whispered.

Liam raised his raven eyebrows, intrigued, and our small party stepped away from the line. I led Liam and Myra toward the back of the house, where there was a patio with a door to the kitchen and great room. We slid open the glass door and finally stepped out of the rain.

The scene that greeted us inside the house was astounding. Every last stitch of cozy, beach-house furniture in the sprawling great room had been cleared away, and in its place were rows of cots, each covered with a plain white sheet. Krista and Lauren moved about, efficiently smoothing bedding and setting up gauze and bandages and bottles of antiseptic on tables. On the far side of the room, the injured streamed in through the front door, where they were checked in and assessed by Police Chief Grantz and the mayor herself. Pete and Cori helped their patient onto a bed nearby.

"Where should I take her?" Liam asked me.

"See the blond woman by the door?" I said, gently rubbing the girl's back. "She'll want to take a look at her."

"Got it," he said, and carried the little girl toward the mayor.

"Come on, Myra. Let's get you a bed," I said.

"I don't want to cut the line," she said a bit uncertainly as she glanced around.

I smiled. "I won't tell if you won't."

We took a step, and Myra listed to the side. Panic gripped me as her eyes rolled up, and I desperately tightened my grip on her, but it was impossible to hold her suddenly lifeless form. Pete noticed and rushed over to help, ducking under Myra's opposite arm.

"What do we do?" I said.

"Here. Get her to the bed." Pete nodded at the nearest cot. Together we staggered toward it and turned around, sitting down with Myra between us.

Myra groaned and her head lolled forward. Then her arm fluttered off my back and she touched her hand to her head.

"What happened?" she asked.

"You fainted. I think."

"You should lie down, but keep your head propped up," Pete said. I shot him a questioning glance. His green eyes were bloodshot and his nose was red. Sweat poured down his face. "My dad was a doctor," he explained to me under his breath. "If you're faint or dizzy, you're supposed to rest but keep your head over your heart."

"Good thing we ran into this nice young man," Myra joked.

I smiled at Pete, who sort of grimaced in return. "Yes.

A very good thing," I said. Pete and I were not the best of friends, considering that not so long ago he and his pal Nadia had accused me of ushering innocents to the Shadowlands. This was the first time I'd spoken to him since Tristan and Nadia had fled, thereby exonerating me and making themselves look guilty as sin. Maybe that was why he currently seemed unable to look me in the eyes.

Once Myra was propped up on a few pillows, she gave me a nod and patted my arm. "Thanks, Rory. You go see if someone else needs your help."

"I'll be back," I promised her. "Thanks, Pete," I added.

But he had already moved on to the next bed to help Cori with another patient.

I turned around to do the same and was immediately overwhelmed by the frenzy of activity. Darcy and Fisher were leading people to cots while some of the older Lifers tended to wounds and complaints. The stream of "survivors" coming through the door was never ending, and I wondered whether we'd even have enough room for all of them. That was when I spotted a pair of people so odd they momentarily took my breath away. Huddled together a few beds from where I was standing were a guy and a girl, about twenty years old, with white-blond hair in the exact same bowl-cut style, their bangs wet and scraggly over their foreheads. Their features were so similar—broad foreheads, straight noses, angular chins—that I might not have guessed their genders except for the fact that the girl was wearing a plain black dress while the boy wore dark pants and a white shirt. They both had light blue eyes and their skin was an olive hue. Their temples were pressed together as they whispered to each other, but their gazes darted around the room, taking everything in. It was eerie—their awkward pose, the way they were communicating so intensely without looking at each other. An eerie, bloodcurdling sort of fear moved slowly through me, the way the fog had engulfed the beach my first night here. Something wasn't right about them. I could feel it.

"Rory!"

I quickly wove my way over to Krista, who was waving me down. She had pulled her blond hair into a low ponytail and was looking a lot less freaked than she had down by the docks. Somehow she'd managed to change into a dry white cotton dress and flip-flops and was setting up an oxygen tank, flipping switches and turning knobs like she'd been doing it every day of her life. I glanced over my shoulder at the creepy twins. They were watching me. I forced myself to turn my back to them. Pretend they weren't there.

"How do you know how to use that thing?" I asked Krista.

She turned to me and shrugged. "I don't. Does it look like I do? Cool."

I snorted a nervous laugh.

"Here. Let's unpack this box of supplies," Krista suggested, lifting a cardboard box onto the nearest bed. "That I know how to do."

"On it."

We tore into the box and pulled out a few first aid kits, some inflatable pillows, and a bunch of ice packs that needed to be chilled. While I worked, I felt the twins' gazes on me, but when I looked over again, they'd gone back to their freaky darting-eyed communication.

"So who's the hottie? I saw you come in with him." Krista nodded toward Liam and the mayor, who were talking over the girl's head near the door. The mayor gestured toward her office and gently took the girl from Liam's arms. Liam watched them go until the door closed behind them, and I breathed a sigh of relief. In five minutes the girl would be done longing for her mom. That was something, at least. At the moment, I was sort of longing for mine, just like I did whenever something awful or confusing happened. But my mother had died over four years ago, well before the rest of us had ever heard of Juniper Landing. At least I knew she was safe somewhere in the Light. She would never be a part of this insanity.

"Only you would ask that at a time like this," I said, half joking.

Her blue eyes widened. "Like you didn't notice? Please."

"His name's Liam Murtry," I told her.

"He saved, like, a dozen people," Krista said, looking him over appreciatively from across the room. "It's like Superman's arrived in Juniper Landing."

"Yeah, he seems pretty perfect. Which probably means he's a psycho ax murderer." I meant it to come out as a light quip, but my tone entirely missed the mark. Who could blame me, though? I was turning out to be a seriously bad judge of character.

Krista fixed a sort of probing look on me.

"What? First my favorite math teacher kills me," I said under my breath. "And then I fall in love with the guy who's taken it upon himself to shift the entire balance of the universe?" I shook my head and took the last roll of gauze out of the box, then ripped the bottom of the box open to flatten it. "From now on, I'm not trusting my instincts about anyone."

I cast a cautious glance over at the twins again. Their temples were still locked, their lips still moving. They gave me the heebie-jeebies, which meant they were probably the loveliest people I'd ever meet in my life. Well, my afterlife.

"I still don't know how everyone is so convinced that Tristan betrayed us," Krista whispered. "I mean, it's *Tristan*. He can't be the bad guy."

"Then where is he, Krista?" I snapped. "Why doesn't he come back and plead his case?"

How could he have done this to us? What could have made him turn on innocent people? On my dad? On me?

Krista was just opening her mouth to respond when her mother and Officer Dorn stepped up behind her. The mayor's thin lips were set in a grim line.

"Girls," the mayor said. "We need to talk."

POLITICIANS

I didn't trust the mayor. Which was only fair, because I was pretty sure she didn't trust me. As Krista and I followed her back into her octagon-shaped office, Joaquin and Dorn fell into step behind us. Good. I felt safer with Joaquin at my back. I glanced over my shoulder at Darcy to make sure she was okay and saw her wrapping an elderly man's ankle with a bandage, chatting with him and smiling. Once we were all inside the office, Dorn pulled the door shut behind us, and the chaotic din of the clinic softened to a dull, continuous hum.

Dorn stood in front of the door, his eyes sharp on me,

his hands clasped before him like a Secret Service agent. Krista and I stood awkwardly in the center of the room, while Joaquin walked over to a leather chair and sat down in it casually, like he owned the place, his ankle resting on his knee. Outside the windows, the storm raged over the ocean, darker and darker clouds gathering. A broken tree branch, its jagged golden insides exposed to the rain, scratched an even tempo on the windowpane behind the mayor's right shoulder.

"What can we do for you, Madame Mayor?" Joaquin asked, folding his arms behind his head.

She shot him a look full of venom, to which he merely cocked an eyebrow, then she sighed. "This has gone entirely too far."

"Nothing like a good disaster to mobilize the local politicians," Joaquin quipped.

"This is not a joke, Mr. Marquez!" she spat. "It's high time we find Tristan and Nadia and find out what the hell is going on around here."

"Oh, so now you believe us?" I asked. The mayor had refused to hear a word against Tristan. She didn't want him to be guilty, so she hadn't listened. I didn't want him to be guilty, either, but I knew what I'd seen. I'd seen the guilt in his eyes when we found his stash of tainted coins, and I'd watched him flee.

The mayor's eyes narrowed at me. "I'm not saying I think Tristan is guilty, but he *has* been here longer than any of the rest of us. He knows things about this island that none of us could possibly know. If anyone has the answers, it's him. Is there still no sign of him or Nadia?"

Joaquin and I shared a hesitant glance. He sat forward, rubbing his hands against his thighs.

"We did find something," he said slowly. "In a cave near the bridge. They were staying there. Very recently."

"What?" Krista asked, paling. Her hand fluttered up to toy with the leather bracelet around her wrist—the same one every Lifer wore. Suddenly my skin started to itch beneath mine.

"And you didn't go after them?" Dorn demanded.

"There was this whole thing where the ferry was sinking?" Joaquin replied sarcastically, rising to his feet. He was just as tall as Dorn and almost as broad. "It kind of seemed more important at the moment."

"Well, put together another search party. Double your numbers," the mayor ordered. "As soon as we get this mess sorted out, you're to go out there and find him. This island is only so big. It's not like they can stay hidden forever."

"Speaking of this mess . . ." Krista said quietly.

We waited for her to finish. Outside, something crashed, and there was a scramble and a shout. The mayor closed her eyes and I saw her lips move as she counted, slowly, to ten. Behind her head, lightning split the dark sky and a boom of thunder shook the house. I gripped the back of the nearest chair as the residual rumbles lingered.

"What *about* it, Krista?" the mayor said finally, impatiently.

"Well, what does this mean?" Krista asked, turning her palms up. "If there's no ferry . . . will people stop coming here?"

Joaquin and the mayor and Dorn looked to one another, as if waiting for someone else to have the answer. But we all knew that no answer was coming. Nothing like this had ever happened before. The mayor and Joaquin had been here longer than Dorn, but even with their century's experience on Juniper Landing, there was no precedent for the mess we were currently in. Finally, the mayor walked around her desk and sat, resting her head against her fingertips, her elbows perched atop a perfectly clean leather desk blotter. She took a breath and then raised her chin.

"I don't know, but if so, I believe it's a blessing," she said.

"A blessing?" Joaquin asked, his face screwed up in consternation. "A blessing that we can't serve our purpose?"

"We couldn't anyway," Dorn put in. "We haven't ushered anyone in days, and the town is at full capacity. We're running out of beds *and* explanations for the weather, the fog, the crowded conditions. . . . Plus there are dangerous criminals walking around among the innocents, so yeah, I'd agree that the loss of the ferry for right now is a blessing."

"But it doesn't mean we can grow complacent," the mayor said firmly. "With the storms and the overcrowding, it's getting harder and harder to keep track of everyone. Do you even know how many charges you currently have on the island?" she asked, looking directly at me.

I pressed my lips together, thinking of the coins that had been appearing on my nightstand on a daily basis, which now sat in a heap at the bottom of the drawer. At first I had been able to keep a mental tally of the souls who had been assigned to my care, but after a few days of chaos, their faces had grown murky in my mind.

"No," I admitted, looking at my feet.

"Do either of you?"

"No," Joaquin and Krista chorused.

The mayor heaved a sigh. "We have to find Tristan. I want every available Lifer on it. We need to fix this situation, and we need to fix it now."

There was a sudden rap on the door. Dorn moved to answer it, but it whipped open before he could get there, and Darcy stepped inside. Her posture slumped in relief when she saw me.

"There you are! It's so insane out there, and you disappeared on me."

She walked right into the room, as if she hadn't interrupted anything, and hugged me. I glanced nervously at the mayor, waiting for the reprimand, but none came. Not even when Liam breached the doorway right after Darcy.

"Um . . . you might want to come out here," he said to the mayor, gesturing over his shoulder. "People are starting to get restless."

She nodded and stood, smoothing her platinum-blond hair over her ears and straightening her fitted suit jacket. Pasting a huge smile on her face, she walked around the desk toward me and my sister. "There is good news, however."

"There is?" I asked, unable to stop myself from stepping protectively in front of Darcy.

"Yes. There is." The mayor looked down her nose at me imperiously, her words clipped. "Darcy, Liam, congratulations! As of today, you are both Lifers. Welcome to the family."

"What?" Krista blurted.

I looked at Darcy, my eyes wide. She, of course, had no idea what was going on. That she would be staying here in Juniper Landing forever—that we'd never be apart. I felt a sudden rush of selfish excitement even as a sort of surprising heaviness settled inside my chest. This also meant she'd never have the chance to move on—to truly be at peace. She'd never go to the Light and see my mom.

How was I ever going to explain her new reality?

"I'm sorry the news must be delivered in this hasty manner. There's usually more subtlety involved," the mayor said. "But under the circumstances, this seems the only way."

I thought back to the way I'd found out—Tristan telling me on the beach that I was dead, then having Fisher knock me out cold when I wanted to tell my family, and waking up in a basement while the whole group of my new friends explained what I was. Not entirely subtle, but I didn't feel like arguing the point.

The mayor shook Darcy's limp hand, then Liam's strong one, and stepped to the door. "You kids will fill them in, won't you?" she said to me, Krista, and Joaquin.

Officer Dorn looked as stunned as the rest of us as he turned slowly and followed her from the room. The door closed with a bang behind them.

"Uh, what was she talking about?" Liam asked, his mismatched eyes wide.

"What the hell is a Lifer?" Darcy asked.

"Um . . . I . . . " How was I supposed to answer that question, exactly?

"Hello? Rory?" She waved one hand in front of my face. "Care to explain?"

I looked into her green eyes, so like my own and my mother's, and took a breath. "Darcy," I said, "I've got good news, and I've got bad news."

There was really no other way to begin.

SISTERS FOREVER

"Are we gonna get to see Mom?" Darcy asked me tearfully.

A lump jammed my throat, and I shook my head. Darcy and I were sitting on the window seat in her bedroom, our hands clasped between us, while Krista and Liam perched on the bed, Fisher hovering near the bottom post. He had insisted on being here for Darcy, so Joaquin had stayed behind at the clinic to take his place with the recovery effort. We had walked back to our house to deliver the news away from the madness, and Darcy had run right upstairs crying after hearing the basics. Both she and Liam had finally calmed down—his reaction had been to try to punch Fisher in the face, which hadn't gone well. Now Darcy had just asked the question I'd been dreading more than any except for one.

"Mom moved on. A long time ago." I took a breath, the pain of this hitting me all over again, and sat amazed at how it seemed to hurt worse each time instead of getting better. "So, you believe me?"

She sniffled and looked down. "He killed us, didn't he?" she asked slowly. "That's how we died—how we got here. Steven Nell killed us."

I nodded, tears spilling down my cheeks.

"Oh my god, Rory."

Darcy flung her arms around me and collapsed. She sobbed, her whole skinny body convulsing as her tears wet my shoulder. I cried as well, feeling the devastation of what had happened to us like a fresh stab wound to the chest. I don't know how long we sat like that, with Liam, Krista, and Fisher silently, respectfully averting their eyes, but I do know that by the time we were done, I was exhausted. She released me, and I leaned sideways against the window, spent.

"So . . . wait," Liam said, speaking for the first time in a few minutes. "You guys were murdered?"

I nodded. "It's a long story."

"That's intense." Liam's brow knit. "How did I die?"

"You drowned, man. Undertow got you." Fisher gave Liam's shoulder an awkward pat.

"Please. There's no way," Liam said. "I'd never drown."

"It's the truth," Fisher said. "If you hadn't become a Lifer, I would have been your usher, so I saw the whole thing when I slapped you on the back before."

"You saw my death?" Liam asked, blanching.

"Just one of the many special powers we Lifers have," Krista said sourly.

"So how did you die?" Liam asked her.

Krista shifted atop the floral bedspread, tugging the hem of her white dress down further over her thighs. "I did something stupid," she said, pursing her lips.

Liam looked around at the rest of us. "Like drowning?" he said lightly, clearly trying to put her at ease.

"No." She glared at him. "I wanted to get my ex-boyfriend's attention, so I took a bunch of pills, but I didn't want to die." Her eyes trailed off to the side as if she couldn't bare to look anyone in the eye right then. "I just . . . took too many."

"Whoa," Darcy said.

"What about you?" Liam asked Fisher. Darcy and I both turned to look at him, curious.

"It was an accident on the football field," he said. "I laid a hit on this guy, and bam!" He slapped one fist into a flat hand. "Neck snapped. Done."

Liam whistled, and I looked Darcy in the eye. He'd just relayed that news like he was going over random stats of a game. Darcy blew out a breath.

"So what happened to him? To Nell?" Darcy asked me.

"You don't remember?"

"I remember now that he was here . . . but how did he get here?"

I cleared my throat. "Well . . . I kind of killed him."

"What?" she blurted.

"You killed a guy?" Liam asked, sliding to the edge of the bed so that his long legs dangled down. "How?"

His eyes were bright—kind of disturbingly bright considering the subject matter. But he had to be a good person to be a Lifer, right?

I turned my shoulder to him and concentrated on Darcy while I told the story.

"I was . . . well, basically I was dying." I paused and took a breath, hating the act of remembering this. "But I got his knife away from him and I . . . "

I trailed off, unable to find a way to complete the sentence that didn't sound like something from a bad horror flick. *I jammed it into his stomach?* No. *I gutted him?* No. Instead, I stared out Darcy's window at the house across the street. The gray house I'd been obsessed with when we first moved here, certain that someone was watching us from its windows. And, of course, I had been right. Tristan had been watching me. Keeping tabs on the new potential Lifer. A horrible, sour burning spread through my stomach as I remembered the day he'd taken me there—showed me the spot from where he'd watched. The day I'd first tried to kiss him and he'd rejected me.

The house was still now. Dark. Like everything else on this damn island.

"Wow. Rory, can we just talk for a second about how badass that is?" Darcy exclaimed, her face still shimmering with tears.

I flinched, my skin tightening. There'd been a time, not so long ago, when it had felt badass. When I'd felt proud of myself for ridding the Earth of the man who killed fourteen girls and took my family as his swan song. But now, it no longer felt that way.

"I don't know," I said.

"Are you kidding me? Just think about the giant favor you did for the world," Darcy said. "Right now there's some random girl running around playing soccer or hooking up with her boyfriend or shopping with her mom, and she's only doing it because you offed the asshole who was coming after her."

"She's right, you know," Krista said. "You're a hero, Rory."

I tried to smile, but I realized, as Darcy eyed me proudly, why I felt so conflicted. Because when I took Steven Nell's life, I hadn't been thinking about the random girls I was saving or even the girls he already murdered. I'd been thinking about me. I'd been thinking about my family and what he'd done to us. And I'd been pissed. I'd slain the man out of revenge, plain and simple. And there was nothing pure or heroic about that. Did I even deserve to be a Lifer?

"What about Dad?" Darcy asked, wiping her eyes and sucking in a loud breath. "Where's he?"

And there was the question I'd been dreading the most. She remembered him, now that she was a Lifer. A few days ago, when he'd moved on, I'd mentioned his name and she'd looked at me like I was crazy. Now her eyes were filled with guarded hope. I didn't want to tell her—didn't need to tell her just yet—about how wrong things were. I decided to keep my answers short.

"He's moved on."

"So Mom and Dad are in the Light."

She didn't ask it, just stated it. And I didn't contradict her. My eyes met Fisher's. He cocked one brow. I shot him a silencing look that I hoped Krista picked up on.

"We're never going to see them again?" she asked, her voice breaking.

I cleared my throat. "No."

She wiped her eyes. "Okay. This is a lot."

"I know," I said. "But the good news is, we're going to be together. Lifers never move on. We'll never have to say good-bye."

Darcy's eyes lit up, and she reached for my hand. "Really?"

I smiled. "Really."

We sat there, clutching each other's fingers and looking out at the rain. Back home, before we died, Darcy and I had been estranged for months—a stalemate over a guy I could barely even remember. She used to love stomping around the house, reminding me and my dad about how very soon she was going to graduate and how she'd be "outta here" without looking back. Then, I couldn't have imagined sitting here with her like this, in peaceful, companionable silence. It was amazing how quickly everything had changed.

"I don't know," she said finally. "Do I really *want* to live with you forever?"

Fisher chuckled. I cracked up laughing and shoved her shoulder. It was a classic Darcy line, and I was glad to see she still had it in her. I knew that I should tell her what had been happening on the island—that my father and others were suffering needlessly in the Shadowlands and we needed to figure out how to get them to the Light—but I didn't want to spoil this moment. The truth of her new existence and the news that she would never see our parents again were enough to take in on one day. I didn't have to scare the crap out of her as well.

For now, I was going to let her process what she'd learned, and I was going to selfishly hold on to this feeling that was sprouting up inside me. This delicate, fluttering white hope that somehow everything was going to be okay.

There was a sudden flash at the corner of my vision—something was moving in the house across the street. I flinched. Then thunder rumbled in the distance, and I unclenched. It had been nothing more than a remote flash of lightning. The storm messing with my head again.

"What I don't get is, why didn't you tell me this before?" Darcy asked. "You've known for . . . how long?"

"A week," I admitted.

"But she couldn't have told you," Fisher said. "And you can't tell any of the visitors. If you do, you damn them to the Shadowlands—and you get sent to Oblivion."

"Seriously? That's a bit harsh," Darcy said, looking over her shoulder at him.

He shrugged. "I don't make the rules."

"So, basically, if I want to relegate some asshole to hell I just have to tell him he's dead?" Liam asked.

Fisher whacked the back of his head so hard his hair stuck up.

"Ow! It was just a joke!" Liam snapped, his face turning bright red.

"We don't joke about stuff like that," Krista said seriously. "Especially Oblivion."

Liam shoved himself up and paced toward the closet. "I just found out I'm dead, okay? Excuse me for trying to lighten the mood."

"Look, it's just that there's some history around here with this stuff. History no one wants to see repeated," I said. "There was a Lifer named Jessica a while back who decided all the visitors deserved to know what was going on, so she told them. Just went around town, knocking on doors and spilling the truth."

"So what happened?" Darcy asked.

"She got every last one of them a one-way ticket to the Shadowlands," Fisher said grimly. "All those innocent people, damned forever."

"For doing nothing wrong," I added.

Lightning flashed again, and Darcy and Liam looked pale. Krista was about to say something when heavy footsteps pounded up the stairs, cutting her off. The floorboards in the hallway groaned, and there was a thudding knock on the door.

"Come in," Darcy said weakly.

Joaquin opened the door, keeping one hand on the knob and one on the doorjamb. "You okay?" he asked her.

"I'll live," she said, then gave a quiet ironic laugh.

"Good." Joaquin's eyes flicked to me. "Mayor's called a Lifer meeting at the police station. We gotta go."

I looked at Darcy, and she endeavored to smile. "Duty calls?"

"Yeah," I said, my stomach curling into knots. "But there are a few more things I'm gonna have to tell you on the way."

So much for giving her time.

EVIL LURKS

"Until further notice," the mayor announced, "the island is on high alert."

An uneasy murmur passed through the hundred or so Lifers gathered in the open area in front of the police station's high front counter. As municipal buildings went, it was fairly small, and we were crowded shoulder to shoulder, some sitting in plastic chairs along the walls, others perched atop the marble counter, and still others—the overflow—hanging out around the officers' desks. I glanced at my friends—Bea, Lauren, Krista, Joaquin, Fisher, and Kevin. No one said it, but we could all feel Tristan's absence. Across the room, Pete and Cori huddled together near a potted palm. Cori's dark curls half covered her face, and her gaze darted furtively here and there as if she thought we were here to accuse her of something. Pete glanced at us and did a quick double take, then pulled his baseball cap low on his head and trained his eyes on the ground. Everyone else was intent on the mayor, who stood at the center of the room with a three-foot radius of open space around her.

"What does that mean, exactly?" the man who ran the grocery stand asked.

Darcy shifted next to me, her arm brushing mine. She had changed into a dry black T-shirt and rolled jeans and stood straight and tall, taking everything in with a discerning, if slightly apprehensive, expression. She had dug out the butterfly necklace my mother had given her for her twelfth birthday and clasped it around her neck. Now she toyed with the pendant, sliding it up and down on the chain. For a girl who'd just had her entire life turned upside down, she was handling it surprisingly well.

"As you know, we've had a watch posted at the bridge for the past four days." The mayor nodded to Officer Dorn and Chief Grantz, who began passing around stapled packets of paper. "From now on we will post similar watches in various spots around the island. Everyone will have a shift or two each day. I want you to keep track of the visitors. Where they go, who they're with, what they're up to. We need your help to keep track of who's here and whether they're ready to move on."

Dorn handed each of us a schedule. Darcy and Liam flipped through theirs, then locked eyes, mutually overwhelmed. I was glad Darcy wasn't the only newbie dealing with this situation. It was good to have someone in the same boat with her.

"You'll see we've also put some of you in charge of the children," the mayor continued. "As of last count, we have eight kids under the age of twelve on the island. They are staying at my house up on the hill, the better to keep them out of danger. Krista has managed to scrounge up some toys and video games from the relic room, and we're planning to set up a playroom in one of our parlors. We need to keep these young souls as innocent as they were the day they arrived here, so if you're in their presence, please, no mention of the unpleasantness we're experiencing."

The chief returned to her side and leaned in to whisper in her ear. Her jaw set, her expression darkened, and she nodded.

"Chief Grantz would also like me to remind you of our *other* special visitors," the mayor continued. "It has been five days since we've moved anyone off this island. We've been concerned about those destined for the Light who might end up in the

Shadowlands, but there are also those souls who belong in the Shadowlands—souls who committed heinous crimes in their lifetimes who should have been moved immediately to their final destinations. Those souls are now roaming free among us. We cannot usher them as hastily as we normally would, because we can't risk them mistakenly ending up in the Light."

She scanned the room slowly, and the murmur rose up again, louder and more urgent this time. I thought of Ray Wagner mocking the survivors this morning and shuddered.

"We must prevent these souls from harming our innocents and ourselves," the mayor said darkly. "To that end, I would like everyone to stay after this meeting and register the names of any soul you are certain was destined for the Shadowlands, so that the rest of us may keep a close watch on them. When we finally rectify the issues we've been having, they will be the first to cross over."

"Why not just lock them up in the jail?" someone shouted.

"We don't have the space," Chief Grantz replied. "Plus we don't want to arouse suspicions by plucking people off the street and locking them up. This is a small island. Word would get around."

"We can control the situation if we stay vigilant," the mayor added.

Darcy turned to me, her eyes wide. "Nell? He's gone, right?"

I grasped her wrist. "Long gone."

She blew out a sigh but didn't look comforted. I couldn't blame her.

Out of nowhere, Joaquin stepped forward to share the circle with the mayor.

"There is some positive news today!" he announced loudly, his voice ricocheting around the room. "Two new souls have proved themselves worthy of being Lifers. Everyone, we'd like you to meet Darcy Thayer and Liam Murtry!"

There was a smattering of applause, which, at Joaquin's cheerleader-type gestures, grew into a rousing ovation as Darcy and Liam waved awkwardly.

"We'll be initiating them tonight, at midnight, at my place," Joaquin continued. "I realize with the new schedule it will be a smaller group than usual, but if you can make it, it'd be good to have you there."

He stepped back next to me again.

"Not the cove?" I whispered.

"In this weather? Personally I'd like to be dry for more than fifteen minutes in a row," he replied under his breath.

I nodded. "Good point. Where exactly is your—?"

The mayor cleared her throat, staring us down. I stopped whispering. "Thank you for that interruption, Mr. Marquez," she said acerbically. "Now, our last but certainly most pressing order of business is to locate Tristan and Nadia and bring them back here for questioning."

The entire atmosphere of the room shifted, and from the pained looks on the faces of those around me, everyone felt it. Tristan was this island's Golden Boy and had been for generations, but by now everyone knew what he'd done. The sense of betrayal was so thick it was suffocating.

"Please check your schedule. If you've been assigned to one of tonight's search parties, see Chief Grantz, who has kindly separated a map of the island into quadrants and will assign one to each party." She paused as papers fluttered and people compared schedules. "If we stick together and do this in an orderly fashion, they will be found and we'll get to the bottom of this mess." She took a deep breath. "Are there any questions?"

The double doors opened suddenly, and a howling wind tore through the station. It was those creepy twins from the clinic. They each wore clear plastic ponchos and had slicked their white-blond hair down and to the side, with opposite parts, so that they looked to be mirror images as they stepped toward the mayor. Their eyes slid left and right, taking in their surroundings. They stayed so close to each other that I assumed they were holding hands, but once they were clear of the crowd I saw this wasn't the case. The backs of their knuckles were merely touching between them.

"Can I help you?" the mayor demanded.

Their scanning eyes snapped forward at the same time and focused on her. "Yes," they said in unison. They lifted their hands to remove their hoods with such perfect timing it looked rehearsed.

Lifers around the room exchanged disturbed glances. Good. I wasn't the only one who was completely wigged out by these two.

"I'm Selma Tse and this is my brother, Sebastian," the girl said in a reedy voice. "There's no Internet, and we can't get cell service, even though our phones were protected inside our bags."

"We just walked through town, and the place is pretty much deserted," Sebastian added. They turned their heads in opposite directions, sliding their suspicious eyes around the room.

"It seems as if everyone is . . . here," Selma said. "Together. The entire town."

"What's the deal with this place?" Sebastian added. "It's not normal."

Thunder rumbled outside. The pendant lights overhead flickered and half the room gasped. I instinctively grabbed Joaquin's arm. Silence.

"I'm sorry, was there a question in there somewhere?" the mayor asked impatiently.

"Yes," Sebastian began, taking a step forward. "Who *are* you people? How did we get here when neither one of us remembers even deciding to leave home? And what the hell is Juniper Landing?"

My fingers dug deeper into Joaquin's arm. Normally the visitors here were programmed to think they were on vacation. They were sort of lulled into a sense of happy complacency. But not these two.

"I knew it," I whispered. "I knew something was off about them."

"Is someone going to answer us?" Selma asked, her voice ringing to the ceiling.

And from the looks in their freaky light eyes, they weren't about to take no for an answer.

THE VANE

I speed-walked across town that night on my way to Joaquin's for Darcy and Liam's initiation, my head bent toward the ground, trying to stay as dry as possible. The sidewalks were crisscrossed with hairline cracks and deep fractures, a spiderweb of hazards in the darkness. Near the corner in front of the general store, one of the gutters was so packed with leaves the water burbled and rose around it, and I saw a dead mouse bobbing up and down on the swell, its eyes blank.

I shuddered and hurried on, wishing Darcy were with me. She'd been assigned to a late shift at the nursery and was meeting me at Joaquin's. It was close to midnight, and the town that was quiet in midday was now graveyard silent, aside from the rain and wind. I saw a stray light illuminated in one of the upper windows of the library. As I was about to dip downhill toward the docks, something in the library window shifted. I paused, heart in my throat, clutching my hood together under my chin. A shadow passed through the light—a person, though it was impossible to tell whether it was male or female.

Maybe I was imagining things. Maybe it was a trick of light. But still, I stood there, alone and shivering, squinting across the rain-flattened grasses of the park. I was just about to call myself crazy and give up, when the figure appeared again. This time, instead of moving on, it squared itself in the window and stood there, staring out. Staring out at me.

Then out of nowhere, a flash of lightning blinded me, and a simultaneous burst of thunder vibrated inside my bones. When I looked up at the window again, the shadow was gone.

I turned around and ran.

Hurdling over fallen branches down the hill, I could feel someone—some*thing*—behind me, gaining on me, tearing with an otherworldly quickness through the night. Wind-tossed leaves swirled up in front of me, and my foot caught on a raised bit of sidewalk, but I righted myself and kept running. Suddenly I heard a sound cut through the rain.

The distant music of the Thirsty Swan, the only business in town still booming. If I could just get there. If I could just find someone, anyone real, maybe I would be okay.

I skidded onto the boardwalk at the bottom of the hill and turned. There was nothing there. Someone grabbed me by the arm.

"Rory?"

I screamed at the top of my lungs, but it was just Liam. He was with a tanned girl with wide dark eyes and long black hair tucked under a poncho hood. The boy walking out the door of the Thirsty Swan and over to join them had to be her brother. He was shorter and tanner, but had the same beautiful eyes.

"Are you okay?" the girl asked me, her face lined with real concern.

I could only imagine how I seemed to her, my breath staggered, my eyes shot through with fear. I must have looked psychotic, haunted.

"I'm fine," I said. "Sorry. It probably wasn't the best idea to walk through the park by myself this late." I extended a shaking, cold, wet hand. "I'm Rory."

"Lalani," she said with a smile, grasping my hand. "This is my brother, Nicholas."

"S'up," the kid behind her said with a nod and a smirk.

"Lalani and Nick were on the ferry, but they swam to

shore on their own," Liam said, looking at Lalani with a proud expression.

"You guys weren't hurt?" I asked.

Nicholas shook his head. "We're from Hawaii, originally. We know how to deal with rough water."

"Hawaii," Liam said giddily. "Isn't that so cool?"

"Awesome," I said, realizing suddenly what was going on here. Liam had a crush. A big one. On a visitor. "You're still going to Joaquin's, right?"

"Oh, yeah. I was just on my way. These guys are headed down to the hotel," Liam said. He turned to Lalani. "So, I'll see you tomorrow afternoon?"

"Rain or shine," she replied, blushing.

Rain. It would definitely be rain.

Liam looked uncertain for a second, like he wanted to kiss her, but then he glanced at me and Nick and thought the better of it. Instead, he raised an awkward hand. "Okay. Bye."

Lalani giggled. "Bye."

Nick rolled his eyes, and they walked off together.

"We're going surfing," Liam said, staring after Lalani until the darkness swallowed her and her brother.

"That's nice," I said as we turned our steps down the alley between the Thirsty Swan and the Crab Shack next door. I had to leap over a puddle the size of a small lake, and Liam followed. "So, crushing on a visitor, huh?"

"Is it that obvious?" he asked.

"Kind of." We skirted a Dumpster and found the set of stairs that supposedly led up to Joaquin's apartment. "Just be careful."

"What do you mean?" he asked as we began to climb. The staircase was slim and rickety, made with whitewashed boards that looked as if they'd been hammered together two centuries ago.

"Just . . . I don't want you to get hurt," I said, realizing in the back of my mind that—considering recent events—I might not be the best person to be giving romantic advice. Or instructions on how to protect his heart. "She's going to be leaving soon. Moving on."

Hopefully, anyway, I added silently.

"Oh. Right." We paused on the tiny landing at the top of the stairs, outside the plain wooden door. He was silent and pensive for a split second before adding brightly, "Or maybe she'll become a Lifer!"

I knocked on the door, smiling in spite of myself. It was nice to have someone around who was optimistic. I could hardly believe that earlier today I'd half suspected him of being an ax murderer. Joaquin opened the door, and his brows knit. He seemed confused at the sight of me and Liam together, but recovered quickly.

"Hey. Come on in."

"How did I not know you live here?" I asked as Liam slipped inside.

"We moved here when we left the house on Sunset. Which you also never visited," Joaquin replied with a teasing grin.

As I stepped over the threshold, I was pleasantly surprised. The living area was long and wide, mirroring the exact space taken up by the restaurant and bar below. A clean, modern kitchen and dining area were separated by half walls and columns from a sunken living room, where couches and chairs were set up in a conversational circle around a coffee table. Candles flickered inside hurricane-style holders, and two doors at the very far end were open to reveal a gray-and-white bathroom and what appeared to be a fairly large bedroom. A hallway led down the right side of the apartment toward the back.

Liam joined Bea, Lauren, and Fisher on the living room couches, where they were chatting as they sipped beer and soda from heavy-looking crystal mugs. Bea's red curly hair was pulled back in a messy bun, as it had been ever since the rain started, and she wore a black-and-gray henley and jeans. Lauren's short, glossy black hair was pushed back with a striped headband, and her blue Juniper Landing sweatshirt was so long it allowed only an inch of her khaki shorts to peek from under the bottom hem. Liam had shed his rain jacket to reveal a deep-burgundy T-shirt with some kind of blown-out logo on it and seriously distressed jeans. A trendy boy, definitely. Fisher was in his usual uniform of dark cargos and a light blue T-shirt so tight I could see every single one of his muscles.

"Hey, guys," I said, handing Joaquin my soaked jacket as he closed the door behind me.

"Rory!" Lauren and Bea cheered.

"Where's Darcy?" Fisher asked, straightening up to better see the door, as if expecting her to suddenly appear.

"She has a shift at the daycare with Krista. She's coming straight from there." I glanced over my shoulder at Joaquin. "Is Ursula home?"

He was reaching up into a high cabinet but turned to nod at the hallway. "She's still not feeling well, so she went to bed early."

The large metal bowl he was pulling out smacked against the top of the cabinet and let out a clang. The baskets underneath it started to spill out.

I reached up to grab the baskets before they could scatter everywhere, and he put the bowl down on the table, which was littered with bags of chips, plastic containers of dip, and some random vegetables.

"Are we having a party?" I asked. "I thought this was an initiation."

"Is it weird?" he asked, showing a flash of uncharacteristic uncertainty. "I just thought, if I'm hosting . . . "

"No," I said, and couldn't help laughing. "It's not weird."

"Good." His arms flexed beneath the short sleeves of his red T-shirt as he started to chop a pepper. I watched his hands as he worked, so adept and sure. It was riveting.

"Where'd you learn to do that?" I asked.

He lifted his hand and sucked a bit of pepper juice off his thumb. "When you cook for yourself for a hundred years, you develop some skills." He nodded toward the dining area. "Could you grab me the wooden platter? It's in the sideboard over there."

"Sure."

For some reason, I felt my heart rate thrumming in my wrists as I moved across the room, and I felt conspicuous. Fisher said something that made Bea and Lauren laugh and Liam blush. No one was paying any attention to me. As I bent to retrieve the platter from a low shelf, I noticed an old scrapbook open on top of the sideboard, its pages browned at the edges. The black-and-white and sepia-toned photos were held to the pages with black corner stickers. The book was flanked by a lit candle on each side, but they were both set a careful distance away from the book. I glanced at the first photo—a grainy shot of a lanky, smiling boy and a younger, round-faced girl in

71

turn-of-the-century clothing—and dropped the heavy platter. It hit the corner of the sideboard with a serious clatter, but I somehow managed to grab it before it fell to the floor.

"God, Rory! Give me a heart attack!" Lauren said, hand to her chest.

"You okay?" Joaquin asked, coming up behind me.

"That's you!" I blurted.

Joaquin nodded. "Yeah. That's me and my sister, Maria."

His sister. The one he'd killed in a car accident. His expression went distant for a moment as he eyed the photograph—not sad, exactly, just not here.

"How did you get this?" I asked. "Did you have it with you when you died?"

It seemed unlikely, considering he'd committed suicide alone in his attic. But the only things any of us had with us in Juniper Landing were those things we'd had on our person when we'd perished. Or in my and Darcy's case, in our bags, since we'd been going into witness protection when Steven Nell attacked.

"No. It was my sister's." He took the platter from me, our fingers grazing. "I found it in the relic room about fifty years ago."

He turned and headed back from the kitchen while my knees almost went out from under me. I placed one hand on the surface of the table and the other on the sideboard to steady myself.

"You *found* it?"

"Crazy, huh?" It was a light statement, but he didn't say it lightly.

Slowly I tried to piece the implications of this together. If it was his sister's and he'd found it in the relic room, then that meant that his sister had come through Juniper Landing when she'd died. When he'd accidentally killed her.

"So she . . . she had it with her when she died?" I asked, joining him in the kitchen.

"She must have brought it to church with her to show her friends," he said as he wiped the platter clean of dust with a wet rag. His eyes flicked to my face. "I know. It's freaky. I've had fifty years to contemplate how freaky it is. I killed her, she came here, and someone ushered her from here and tossed her stuff in the relic room only for me to stumble on it decades later when I was looking for a new needle for my turntable. I know."

His hands started to shake as he wiped the platter yet again. I reached out and put my hand on his wrist, steadying him. He stopped moving.

"Does anyone remember her? Did Tristan . . . ?"

I paused, his very name on my tongue causing my mouth to dry out. Joaquin shook his head. "No one really remembered her. I like to think it was because she was ushered straight to the Light." His eyes shone as he looked at me, and he smiled. "She didn't exactly have any unfinished business to deal with. That was all mine."

My free hand fluttered to my chest. "Joaquin, I'm so—"

"Don't." He turned and put the platter down. "Seriously, don't. It's fine. I mean, it's not fine, but it is what it is." He glanced across the room at the album and lifted a shoulder. "I'm glad I have it. It's filled with good memories. And without it I'd have no images of anyone in my family, so . . . "

"Wow."

For a moment, I couldn't imagine the right thing to say. Joaquin stood still, his fingers pressing into the top of the kitchen island, the tips going white.

"Are you guys ever gonna bring the food in here?" Bea demanded. "I'm starving."

I hurried to grab a bag of chips, then emptied it into a basket. Joaquin added the chopped vegetables to the platter and followed behind me.

"What were you guys talking about in there?" Fisher asked. "It looked pretty serious."

"I was just telling Rory about some of the weirder visitors who've come through here," Joaquin answered quickly, shooting me a *go with it* look as he set the platter down on the table. Bea darted forward and grabbed a handful of veggies before anyone else could move.

"Um, yeah," I said. "Like those twins from the station? Totally weird."

Lauren shivered, her hair shimmering in the candlelight. "I know, right? Those two give me the willies. I hope Chief Grantz was able to explain everything."

"If not, can't the mayor just wipe their memories?" I asked.

"Wait. The mayor can wipe people's memories?" Liam said, sitting forward.

"To a degree," Joaquin answered, sitting down on an empty love seat. "She only does it in extreme situations, when someone's behavior threatens the peace or our cause."

There was nowhere else for me to go, aside from the floor, so I sat next to him, leaning into the opposite arm.

"So why doesn't she just wipe everyone who came in on the ferry today?" Liam asked. "That's an extreme situation."

"Because she gets sick if she does it too much," Bea explained, tugging on one of her errant curls and wrapping it tightly around her finger. "It takes a lot out of her."

"Really? I never knew that. Like how?" I asked.

"Like if she wiped the whole ferry, she'd probably put

herself in a coma," Fisher said, crunching into a carrot stick. "So you could see how it's better to try to deal with people in a non-mind-meld way first."

I blew out a sigh. "Wow. I guess every superpower has its limits."

We sat in silence for a moment, until Lauren sat forward and grabbed some vegetables. "Remember Andy Warhol?" she asked, changing the subject abruptly. "That guy was nuts."

"And Babe Ruth?" Joaquin shot back. "He was an animal."

Liam's jaw dropped. "You met Babe Ruth?"

"And ushered him," Joaquin said with a laugh. "But only after he got me good and drunk."

"What about you?" Joaquin asked, popping a cucumber slice into his mouth. "Who was the weirdest person you ever met?"

I instantly thought of Steven Nell, but I wasn't about to go there. "There was a kid at my school who could relate any situation in life back to *Star Wars*."

"Seriously?" Fisher asked. "Like how?"

"Like this one time I had a fight with my dad and I was telling a friend about it, and this kid walked up to me and said, 'At least he didn't chop your hand off with a light saber,' then walked away."

Everyone laughed. "No way," Lauren said.

"Yep." I grinned and took another chip. "And then there

was this girl who swore she was going to be a supermodel one day, so she walked around school for three years with a stack of books balanced on her head."

"Was she hot?" Joaquin asked.

"Nope. Not even a little bit," I replied, cracking up.

Liam's brows knit. "What kind of crazy-ass school did you go to?"

Everyone laughed. I leaned back in the love seat and just let myself feel the joy of that one brief moment. Inside that cozy apartment with those people, there was nothing wrong in the world. We were just a few friends having fun.

"It feels good to laugh," I commented.

"Yeah." Joaquin looked me in the eye. "We should do this more often."

My skin humming, I held his gaze, refusing to look away. Then Fisher cleared his throat.

"Where the hell is Darcy?"

The spell was broken. I glanced at my watch. It was twelve seventeen.

"Could she have gotten lost?" Liam asked.

"She knows where the Thirsty Swan is," I said, immediately regretting my sarcastic tone. Liam had been here less than a day. He didn't need me biting his head off for making perfectly acceptable assumptions. "Sorry."

I got up and walked to the door, peering out the window

beside it. Which of course showed me nothing but the side of the next building across the alleyway.

"Maybe she had to stay late," Joaquin suggested, coming up behind me.

"Or maybe she was attacked by one of our resident criminals." I reached for my coat.

"Where're you going?" he asked.

"I'm gonna walk up to the mayor's," I said, flipping the still-wet hood up over my hair. "Hopefully I'll bump into her on the way."

"I'll go with you." He took his jacket down as well and slipped his arms into the sleeves. I started to turn him down but held my tongue. There was no reason to go out there alone.

"You want us to come?" Fisher asked.

"It's okay. You stay here in case she shows," Joaquin said, zipping up his jacket. "You can tell Liam a little more about what he's in for."

"Great," Liam said enthusiastically. "Because I have a ton of questions. Starting with Babe Ruth . . . "

"Hopefully we'll be right back," I said. Then I led Joaquin back out into the rain. "Sorry," I said as we were instantly drenched. "You didn't get your fifteen minutes of dry."

"Maybe later," he replied.

We made our way down the creaking, swaying steps and

through the alleyway. The boardwalk that ran along the bay and was fronted by various restaurants and businesses was deserted aside from the Swan, which was full of voices, music, and clinking glasses. We turned the corner and started up the hill toward town, Joaquin walking behind me on the narrow stretch of sidewalk. Every second, I kept hoping Darcy would appear at the top of the hill, and each moment that she didn't, my pulse started to race a bit faster. Finally, out of breath and scared, we reached the top of the hill.

We were standing at the southwest corner of town, close to the ferry dock. The scent of burned wood still hung in the air. The park at the center of town was empty, and my eyes darted to the suspicious library window. It was dark.

"She isn't here," I said.

There was no reply other than the rain pattering against my hood. It was a sound I was getting seriously sick of hearing.

"So we'll walk up to the clinic," Joaquin said casually, though his eyes were darting over the town square with concern. "I'm sure she's there."

Before the words had completely faded into the air, something in the atmosphere changed. My heart hit my throat as I realized that the fog overhead was moving. Since we hadn't ushered anyone in days, the fog had become constant, but instead of surrounding us in an endless whiteout, it hung like an ominous and solid cloud two stories above our heads, giving the town the illusion that it had been topped off by a thick blanket of gray cotton candy. But now the mist swirled and withdrew, pulling back over the island like the lid of a huge picnic basket sliding open to reveal the luscious wonders inside. The rain still fell, but the clouds overhead were spotty, and stars shone through in the black sky. I looked across the town and saw rooftops and spires I hadn't seen in what felt like forever, lights at the tip-tops of buildings, and the bridge far off to the northwest.

"Wow," I breathed. After days of murky, creepy darkness, nothing had ever seemed so beautiful.

Then Joaquin's hand clasped my forearm, his fingers contracting into my flesh. "Rory."

The realization slammed into me like a truck. If the fog was rolling out, someone had been ushered.

"Ohmigod."

We rushed to the edge of the sidewalk and looked up at the bluff on the far end of the island where the mayor's house sat overlooking the town. The weather vane atop the highest peak spun wildly on its axis, as if struggling with tornado-force winds. Then, suddenly, it slammed to a stop, the gold swan shivering against the clouds.

My heart dropped into my toes. The vane pointed south.

One hand reached up to cover my lips. *Not again. Please not again.*

"It's not done," Joaquin said.

The vane had started to spin once more, but this time it stopped much quicker. Again, it pointed south, straight and true. Two more souls had been sent to the Shadowlands.

Tristan and Nadia were back in business.

PRIMAL

Mud splashed along the side of the road as Joaquin's pickup truck navigated the bumps and craters created by the storm. I clung to the handle just over my head, my teeth grinding together as I held my breath.

How had they done it? How had they gotten past the search parties and the guards and managed to grab two innocent visitors and usher them? And why? Why take more? When was it ever going to be enough?

Wet, twisted reeds slapped against the passenger-side door as the raindrops wound across the window. When I looked out at the lights shimmering downtown, it looked so peaceful, as if everything was exactly as it should be. Except it wasn't. Not at all.

Suddenly Joaquin jammed on his brakes. I flew forward, the seat belt locking into place one second too late and nearly choking me.

"Shit."

Joaquin jammed the shift into park and threw open the door with a loud creak. I squinted through the windshield as the wipers continued to *thwap* like mad, and gasped. There was a body in the road.

I clambered out the door and raced to Joaquin's side. He was crouched over the prone form of one of the librarians, a thick man I'd seen walking around town with all manner of books tucked under his arms. He had a bushy mustache and small, silver-framed glasses, which had been tossed aside in the muck.

"Willis? Willis, are you okay?" Joaquin shook his shoulder.

I heard a groan behind me and saw another man lying on the road. He was unfamiliar but dressed in the same yellow parka as Willis's. I ran over to him as he lifted his head, and helped him sit up. His fingers fluttered up to touch his skull, where a huge lump protruded through his thinning blond hair.

"What happened?" I asked, holding him up.

"I don't know. Someone jumped us from behind. I didn't see a thing." He blinked up and squinted at the clouds moving at a fast clip across the starry sky. "The fog! Someone was ushered?"

"Looks that way," Joaquin muttered.

I glanced around, trying to find footprints, tire tracks, anything that could help us figure out where Tristan and Nadia had gone after they'd done the deed. That was when I saw a glint in the light at the edge of the headlight beams. I shoved a soaked lock of hair off my face and crawled for it. I was inches away when I realized what it was, and my vision began to swim. I sat down hard on my hip, a choking noise escaping my lips.

No. It couldn't be. No, no, no.

"Rory? What is it?" Joaquin asked.

I reached out for the delicate gold chain. One wing on the tiny butterfly was dented and the chain was broken.

"It's Darcy's," I said flatly as Joaquin shone a flashlight over the necklace. I pushed myself to my feet, quaking from head to toe as my fist closed around the chain. "It's Darcy's, Joaquin!" I whirled on Willis and his partner, my eyes nearly popping from my skull. "Did you see her? Did you see my sister?"

The librarian shook his head, his jaw hanging low. He seemed shell-shocked, as if he hardly understood what I was saying.

"Joaquin, can a Lifer be ushered?" I asked, tears stinging my eyes as sobs packed my throat. "They can't, can they? Tell me they can't."

"She . . . isn't technically a Lifer. Not yet."

"What?" I blurted.

"You don't become a Lifer until you choose our way. Until you get the bracelet and are initiated. Darcy's still . . . "

"A visitor," I breathed.

"Rory." Joaquin's voice cracked, and he stopped.

"No," I said, my vision blurring. "No. This can't be happening. It can't." I took a shaky step back toward the bridge, where the fog still swirled, as always, around its entrance. "Darcy!" I screamed. "Darcy, can you hear me?"

The only reply was the hissing of the mist.

"Darcy, please! Please answer me! Please!"

I fell to my knees, clutching the necklace and sobbing through my uselessness. Deep inside, I knew it was pointless. I knew there was nothing I could do. She was already gone. My heart tore at the thought of Darcy in pain. Darcy afraid. Darcy in the Shadowlands. Tristan had taken my father and now my sister. Why? Why was he doing this to us?

He probably thought I was too weak to fight back. Too new. Too helpless and confused and scared. But he was wrong. He'd awakened something inside me. Something primal and protective and determined. I could feel it building

85

up in my gut, filling my heart with pure red anger, making my fingertips itch for something to claw at, something to strangle, something to maim. I clutched the butterfly until its wings pierced my flesh and turned around slowly to face Joaquin.

"Find him," I said through my teeth.

"We will," he promised me. "I swear to you, we will."

"Good. And when we do, he's mine." I shoved the necklace into my pocket and stalked past them toward the truck.

"What're you going to do to him?" Willis asked tremulously.

"I'm going to give him exactly what he deserves," I said, yanking open the door. "I'm going to send him straight to Oblivion."

SUCCESS

I kneel on the ridge just out of view and watch. I watch Rory fall to her knees. Watch her spit and shout and swear. Watch her storm to the truck and slam the door. Little Rory Miller's pissed as hell, and I'm loving every minute of it. I mean, taking Darcy was a stroke of genius. Just when she thought she and her sister could make a perfect little after-life for themselves here, I took it away. If she wasn't invested enough before, she will be now.

She's playing perfectly into my hands.

A NOTE

The next morning, I stood shivering inside the mouth of the cave beneath the bridge, my face tight and dry from lack of sleep, feeling the emptiness of the place in every inch of my bones. Clearly Tristan and Nadia had abandoned this particular hideout. Clearly they were never coming back.

Joaquin and Fisher stepped up on either side of me and flicked on their flashlights, joining the beams with my own. Bea, Lauren, Cori, and Pete brought up the rear. Every one of us wore head-to-toe raingear, and the mud that had splattered up our legs and covered our shoes made us look like a group of ragtag roadside-ditch workers. Bea had on a weathered Dodgers cap over her red hair, while Lauren wore a bright yellow Paddington Bear–style rain hat that hid her face down to her nose. Pete's hair was so wet the normally red locks looked black. Cori leaned against him with gray smudges beneath her eyes and her dirty hair tied into two haphazard braids.

"Why are we here, again?" Pete asked. I noticed bandages on several of his fingers as he pushed his hood back, and the prominent Adam's apple in the center of his long neck bobbed when he talked. "I sincerely doubt they're here waiting for us."

"It's the last place we know for sure Tristan and Nadia stayed, and they left some stuff behind," Joaquin said. "It might be a long shot, but we've gotta search it for clues."

"So let's do it," Fisher said, his voice a mere croak. Even though it was pitch-black in here, he wore dark sunglasses that hid what I'm sure were bloodshot eyes. My heart went out to him. I imagined he'd spent the night the same way I had, tossing and turning, waking from horrible dreams of Darcy being tortured, Darcy terrified, Darcy alone, alone, alone.

I'd taken the spare bed in Krista's room, not wanting to go back to my empty house by myself, and this morning she'd told me I'd been crying out in my sleep. So even when I'd thought I was resting, I clearly wasn't.

"Back there." Joaquin pointed, and we followed Fisher inside, forming a long, snaking single line.

Fisher had to duck considerably until we made it into the widest chamber, and even then the ceiling was so low he had to crouch. I flashed my beam toward the back of the cave and froze. The tools, food, and clothing that had been there yesterday were gone.

"They came back for their stuff!" I blurted.

"What?" Joaquin moved quickly to the spot and looked around. The place was empty. "Damn, T. You've got some balls, I'll give you that."

"How can you take this so lightly?" I demanded. "They must have known we'd been here, and they still came back?"

"It's like they're taunting us," Bea agreed.

"Spitting in our faces," Pete said, his breath short.

"You guys! I found something."

Cori crouched at the spot where my flashlight beam had come to rest, and tugged something out of a crack in the wall. It was a tiny piece of paper, rolled up into a tight tube. As she unrolled it, Fisher went to stand next to her, holding his light over the page. They gave it a quick glance, and Fisher paled. Cori's eyes darted uncertainly to me, like she suddenly found me very intimidating.

"What is it?" Lauren asked.

Cori cleared her throat. "It's for Rory," she said meekly,

holding the paper out in my direction but training her eyes on my shoes.

My pulse pounded in my very fingertips as I took the fragile page from her. Instantly, I recognized Tristan's handwriting. My eyes darted over the scrawled lines, falling on key words like *trust, father,* and *love.*

"What's it say?" Lauren asked, stepping up next to me to read over my shoulder.

"'Dear Rory. I didn't do this.'" My voice was cracking already. I coughed and continued to read. "'I didn't do this. Those coins were planted in my room. I keep seeing the look on your face that day in my bedroom, and it's killing me, knowing you don't believe me.'"

My voice caught and I realized this wasn't going to work. I shoved the page at Lauren and covered my face with my hands. He was lying. He had to be. First he'd taken my father, then my sister, and now he was trying to win me back. But why? Why was he doing this to me?

"'I will do anything to regain your trust,'" Lauren read slowly, quietly. "'I'm going to find a way into the Shadowlands. I'm going to get your father and Aaron and the others back if it kills me.'"

She paused and I pulled my quivering hands down, watching her as she finished.

"'I love you,'" she read. "'Tristan.'"

The page fluttered as Lauren handed it back to me. I pocketed it quickly, hugging myself as tightly as I could to stop the shaking, and glanced up at Joaquin. He looked as if he'd just seen a ghost.

"He didn't risk coming here to get his stuff," Bea said, her voice barely a whisper. "He risked coming here so he could leave that for you."

"He's telling the truth," Lauren said firmly. "He's trying to fix things."

"You don't know that." I didn't mean to snap, but I did. A by-product of the tension that was begging for any kind of release. "You only want to believe it."

"Look at the note again," Lauren said, gesturing at my pocket. "He didn't mention your sister."

"So?"

"So, if he was doing this, he'd know your sister had gone over, too. He'd have included her," Lauren asserted.

"Not if he was being smart," Fisher pointed out. "Not if he realized a person who'd fled five days ago wouldn't know about Darcy."

"I can't take this anymore," I cried, holding my hands to my head, feeling as if it was about to split in two. "I can't."

"We have to find them," Fisher said.

Bea sighed. "But we've looked everywhere. We've searched every inch of the island. It's not like he went back to the mainland," she added sarcastically. "So unless he's hiding underwater somewhere . . . "

I felt something catch in the back of my mind. We *had* searched every inch of the island, because the island was the entire world in this in-between. Except, of course, that it wasn't. There was the water. And the things that traveled over the water. Like the ferry, the Jet Skis, the surfboards and kayaks and canoes. And there was also one particularly foreboding structure that stood above the water. A place where no Lifer would ever think to look, because no Lifer had ever stepped foot on it for more than ten seconds.

There was the bridge.

ON THE BRIDGE

"You're out of your mind, you know," Joaquin called after me as I trudged through hollows and puddles toward the bridge. I had climbed up the cliff in record time, my adrenaline spurring me to inhuman feats of strength and daring, but Joaquin had stayed right on my heels. If any of the others had decided to follow us, they hadn't yet made it to the top. "What, exactly, do you think this is going to accomplish?"

I ignored him and kept walking. Up ahead, I saw that Officer Dorn was stationed at the bridge with Liam. They did a double take when they saw me coming and moved to intercept me.

"Hey," Liam said, lifting a hand. His new Lifer bracelet was caught on the end of his sleeve, the leather hard and pristine. Last night, after Darcy had gone missing, Joaquin, Lauren, and Bea had given him what I'd heard was the quickest initiation ever.

"Where the hell do you think you're going?" Dorn asked, stepping in front of me.

I lifted my face, letting the rain sluice down it and along my neck. "I'm going to find the entrance to the Shadowlands."

Dorn laughed. At that moment, Joaquin caught up to me.

"Are you kidding me?" he asked, his dark eyes desperate. "You can't do that!"

"Why not?" I demanded. "Has anyone ever tried?"

Joaquin crossed his arms over his chest, the rivulets of water forming new patterns down his sleeves. "Not that I know of. I mean, I've gone a few steps into the mist when a visitor is giving me trouble, but that's about it."

"So? Then how do you know I can't do it?" I gritted my teeth and took a breath, trying to stay calm. If I got hysterical right now, they'd never let me cross. "We've searched the entire island for Tristan and Nadia, right?"

"Yeah," Dorn replied. "Two or three times already."

"So what if they're *on* the bridge?" I asked, my heart skipping erratically. "It's the only place no Lifer ever goes, and I'd bet that Tristan is counting on that—counting on our fear of the unknown to keep him safe. What better place to hide than the one place no one in their right mind would ever look?"

Liam raised his hand as if he were hoping to be called on in class. "I know I'm new to this stuff, but that does sound about right."

Joaquin's whole expression shifted. He looked at me as if dumbfounded and impressed at the same time. Which was kind of nice.

"Rory," he said slowly. "You're a genius."

"Wait a minute, now," Dorn began.

"Let's do it," Joaquin said, with a giddiness in his tone that I hadn't heard before.

Dorn lifted both his meaty hands. "Uh-uh. No way."

"You're coming with me?" I asked Joaquin, ignoring Dorn. My terror melted away to more of a simmering nervousness. I knew I had to do this, but having company seemed like a good idea.

"Like I'd really let you snag the glory." He smiled shakily.

"I hate to burst your bubble, but you two aren't going anywhere," Dorn barked.

There was a rumble of thunder in the distance, and we looked up at the sky. A drop of rain fell like a dart into my right eye. It stung like acid. I pressed the heel of my hand into it and blinked it away.

"Think about it, Dorn," Joaquin said, getting right in the man's face. "How big of an idiot would you feel like if you found out Tristan was sitting ten feet away from you and you didn't know it?"

"I know I'd feel like a *huge* idiot," Liam put in helpfully.

There was a beat as Dorn narrowed his eyes. He was going to say no and have us escorted back to town or something. I couldn't let that happen. Not when I was so sure we were this close. This close to finding Tristan, to getting my dad back, to saving Darcy.

"If we find him, we'll let you take the credit," I offered.

Dorn titled his head. I could see the glint in his eyes as he imagined delivering the news to the mayor that he had apprehended Tristan. "Yeah?"

"Sure. Why not?" Joaquin confirmed.

He frowned, considering, and the rain picked up, pinging off his broad shoulders.

"Okay, fine. You can go."

"You bet your ass we can go," Joaquin said, starting past him.

"Thank you!" I put in.

At that very moment, the rest of our posse showed up, breathless from the climb and soaking from head to toe. Fisher had removed his sunglasses and looked seriously pissed. Pete took one look at our belligerent stances and trained his eyes on the ground, his hood covering his face. The others hung back a bit as Fisher and Bea stormed over to us.

"*What* are you guys doing?" Bea asked, her hands on her hips.

"Searching the bridge for Tristan and Nadia," Joaquin said, raising his eyebrows. "Wanna come?"

They all seemed to protest at once, but Joaquin and I ignored them and strode purposefully toward the bridge, Cori, Pete, and Lauren close behind us. We stepped up to the very lip, where its metal surface met the dirt of the road, and I stopped breathing.

The entrance was entirely obscured by swirling fog. The eerie hiss of the mist sent a shiver right through me. I pressed my fists together in front of me to try to keep myself from shaking noticeably.

You can do this, I told myself. I couldn't even imagine how the bridge had looked to my father and Darcy. At least I had a choice. They had been dragged over against their will, terrified, probably screaming for help.

Joaquin and I looked at each other. He had my back. I could see it in his eyes. My fingers suddenly itched to hold his hand.

"You guys! Don't do this!" Bea said, storming over to us. She shoved her hood off her hair to look us in the eye. "You have no idea what might happen to you. Good people are getting sent to the Shadowlands. How do you know you're not just going to get sucked in there, too?"

"We don't," Joaquin said.

Lauren whimpered and cuddled into Fisher's side. He covered his mouth with one hand, and even from a few yards away I could see that he was shaking. Cori paced back and forth, gnawing on her lower lip.

"I can't be here for this," Pete said, pulling his hood on as he stepped back and away from the group. "I can't look."

With his head down he marched off, Liam watching his back as he went. Liam was the only person who didn't seem completely disturbed by what we were doing. Which made sense, since he could never have grasped the real gravity of the situation. He'd never seen anyone go over the bridge, never ushered anyone himself, never experienced the horror I'd felt when Aaron had gone to the Shadowlands after I'd sent him on his merry way. To him, this was just a creepy bridge. He'd never seen firsthand what it could do.

"I have to do this, Bea," I said quietly. "If there's a chance he's on the bridge, I have to find him. I have to help my family."

Bea's eyes suddenly flooded with tears. "Don't. Rory, you don't—"

I reached out and squeezed her hand. "It's going to be okay," I told her, barely believing it myself.

She looked desperately at Joaquin, but Fisher was the one who spoke up. "Jay, you're not really going to do this. You're not seriously going to tell me you think this is a good idea."

"It may not be a good idea, but it's the only idea we've got," he said.

He reached over to take my hand and gave it a squeeze. My heart flooded and a faint blush crept up my cheeks. "You ready?" he asked.

I nodded, even though, of course, I wasn't. "Let's go."

"No," Lauren cried. "You guys! No! Don't do this! Don't—"

We took our first step into the wall of fog, and her frantic pleas were cut off. It was as if someone had hit a cosmic mute button and the world went silent, save for the mist. I took a breath. The fog undulated as I exhaled. Joaquin's arm was warm and steady. He gave me a bolstering look.

"Okay?" he said.

"Okay."

We took another slow, tentative step. Then a third, a fourth, a fifth. The air grew markedly colder with each breath. Joaquin adjusted his grip on my hand, and

I could feel the slick sweat that had pooled between our palms.

"Tristan?" he called loudly, clearly.

There was nothing. Nothing but the hissing of the mist. We walked a bit farther, and I realized suddenly that it wasn't even raining here in the murky grayness. The bridge was immune to the weather. Except for the fog.

"Tristan?" I said, then gulped. "Nadia?"

It was worth a try, but there was no response. My spine crawled, and I steeled myself, holding on tighter to Joaquin's hand. Even if they were here, they wouldn't be able to see us any better than we could see them. Right?

We took another tentative step. Another. And then we heard the laugh—and the whispering. Joaquin and I froze.

" . . . look at them . . . "

" . . . she thinks that she's . . . "

" . . . can't even . . . "

" . . . dead . . . "

A cold dread settled in my bones. I stood, holding my breath and listening.

"Who's there?" Joaquin said at full voice.

The response was a single, sarcastic laugh. Male, female—I couldn't tell. All I knew was that it was laughing at me. Then, a single icy finger trailed ever so slowly down the back of my neck. I gasped and then realized with a sinking feeling that I was no longer holding Joaquin's hand. It was as if someone had grabbed him from behind and dragged him away so fast he didn't even have time to scream.

"Joaquin!" I shouted. "Joaquin!"

The mist gathered around the spot where he'd stood, forming into a perfect wall as if he'd never even been there. Hot tears of terror coursed down my face.

"Joaquin! Where are you?" I could still feel the warmth of his fingers against mine. "Where are you?"

Silence, as complete and total as death. My fingernails drilled into my palms. I was alone.

Someone blew on my neck. I let out a screech and whirled around. Nothing but the mist.

"Stop it. Please," I whimpered. "Please. Please don't hurt him. I just want to find my sister. My dad. Please just leave us alone."

"Rory!" a voice sang out teasingly. "Rooooreeee!"

And then, the whistling. "The Long and Winding Road." It was being whistled directly into my ear.

I ran for my life, forgetting everything other than my own survival. I sprinted straight ahead—away from the voice—barreling through the fog, certain at every moment that I would run right into the waiting arms of my tormentor, Steven Nell. I looked over my shoulder, to the left, to the right. There was nothing but the mist. The unforgiving, unrelenting mist.

As I kept running, an awful thought began to scratch at the back of my mind. What if I ran right into the Shadowlands? But no. It wasn't possible. I needed a coin to open the portal. My only hope was to stay on the bridge. To keep going. If I kept going, maybe I'd find Joaquin or Tristan or Nadia—someone. Anyone who could tell me how to find my way back.

I was panting. About to pass out. How long had I been running? How long did I have to go before I—

"Rory, honey, stop."

"Mom?"

I tripped. My knees hit the metal roadway with a jarring slam. I gasped in relief. I'd heard my mother's voice. I'd *heard* her. I sucked in a few breaths, my lungs on fire, and tried to focus, pressing my palms into the grooved metal ground. I took comfort in its very existence. At least it was familiar. It was something real.

"Mom?" I pushed myself up again, turning around in circles. "Mom?"

" . . . which way is she . . . "

" . . . doesn't know . . . "

" . . . so naive she is, so very . . . "

" . . . straight ahead, honey. Straight ahead."

Something moved in the mist, and I ran toward it. "Joaquin?" I paused and gathered myself, squinting. Suddenly I smelled something familiar. The spicy scent of Tristan's shampoo. I felt his presence as clearly as if he were standing beside me, holding my hand. It was as if I could hear his heartbeat.

"Tristan?" I said, my voice cracking. "Tristan, is that you?"

There was a clearing up ahead. I could almost see. Was it the portal to the Light? The Shadowlands? Was it Joaquin? Tristan? Was my mother really here? I ran as fast as I could, holding on to hope, trying to blot out the fear. But as I ran, something pulled at my hair. Not the fog, not the rain, but something alive. Long, hungry fingers reached for me, snagging in my hair, trying to drag me back. The harder I ran, the farther they reached, now scratching at my ears, now whisking against my cheeks.

" . . . don't go, don't go, we can't let you go . . . don't go, don't go, we can't let you go . . . "

"Help me!" I screeched. "Someone, help me!"

I stumbled forward, my lungs burning. All I could feel were my feet pounding the ground and fear coursing through my veins. I ran and I ran and I ran until the rain suddenly battered my face—and I collided with Joaquin.

"Rory?" he said, grasping my elbows. "Oh my god. I thought I'd lost you."

"You're here!" I threw my arms around him and hugged him. "You're all right!"

Joaquin cupped the back of my neck with one hand and tilted his head into my hair. "It's okay. You're okay."

When I finally got control of myself, I looked up, over his shoulders. The others were still standing there, in the exact same poses they'd been in when we left. I looked over my shoulder at the bridge, disoriented. I'd run in a straight line, hadn't I? How could I have come back to the exact spot I'd left?

"I don't understand," I said, grasping Joaquin's jacket as I tried to calm my racing thoughts. "How long were we gone? How long were we in there?"

"Three seconds," Bea replied. "What the hell did you see?"

Joaquin and I locked eyes. I shook my head. I'd run for at least five minutes. Maybe ten. After three years of cross-country races I knew how to judge the length of my run.

"He wasn't there," I said, unable to imagine trying to explain what had gone on inside the mist. "He wasn't . . . He wasn't there."

Joaquin held me to him, his arms locked tightly around me as the rain consumed us. Then, through my wet lashes, I saw a flash of pink, and suddenly Krista was running through the muck in our direction.

"Krista? What's wrong?" Bea called out.

"The mayor sent me to get you. She's losing it, guys," Krista said, gasping for breath as she braced her hands over her knees. "You better come back. Like, now."

THE POLITICIAN

Standing under the same white party tent we'd used for Krista's anniversary party almost a week ago, which had been erected over the flagstone patio behind the mayor's house, we could hear the patients inside getting ready to move out. Between the pane dividers on the French doors, I saw the mayor hovering over a map of the town with a few visitors, explaining where to go as a group headed to the front door. The clinic was emptying.

"Dude, your boy's on the prowl," Fisher said, tilting his head toward the side of the house.

Joaquin walked around to see better, and I automatically

went with him. Jack Lancet, one of Joaquin's more evil charges, was pacing outside one of the east-facing windows, looking through the panes with a creepy smile on. The man had been executed after murdering three helpless children.

"Sonofa—"

Joaquin stormed right over to him, grabbed him by the back of his coat, and flung him away. Lancet hit his knees, muddying the front of his pants, and looked up at Joaquin with pink shame painted across his cheeks.

For a split second, I felt sorry for him. He looked sad, almost disgusted with himself, as he cowered in the rain. Part of me wanted to go help him up, offer him a kind word. But then my logical side kicked in.

The guy is sick, Rory. Sick. He hurt—killed—little kids.

It was that one word that wedged itself inside my chest, though, and stuck, like something jagged and raw. *Sick.* Who was to say what made people do the things they did? Was it nature? Nurture? Their own logic? Their needs and their longings? What had made me kill Steven Nell that day? Why was it my instinct to lash out and take his life rather than to turn the other cheek?

This horrible ache settled deep inside me, and I longed for my mother and the comfort of her words in a way I hadn't in a long time. At the same moment, I wished like hell that Tristan had made good on his promise to be there for me, to be trustworthy, to teach me everything I needed to know. He'd been doing this for so long that I was sure he had the answers to my deep, dark questions.

What if he'd been telling the truth in that note? What if there was still a chance . . . ?

Suddenly Jack Lancet looked me in the eye and laughed. I felt my face harden, my jaw clench. It was as if he'd read my mind and was laughing at my naive hope.

Tristan was evil. I wouldn't give him the chance to fool me again.

"Get the hell out of here," Joaquin growled at Lancet. "We don't want any trouble from you."

Lancet pulled his lapels up around his chin and scurried off in a zigzag line, his laughter carrying back to us on the wind. I peeked through the window and saw two boys playing video games, a few little girls—including Darcy's charge—busy with a tea party, and a handful of others reading books and stacking blocks. Krista's makeshift playroom. Suddenly I went dizzy.

"I think I'm gonna be sick," I said, touching a hand to my head.

Joaquin gently took my hand. "It's okay. They're safe. For now, anyway."

Still, I made sure to watch Jack Lancet until he was finally down the hill and out of sight. When we rejoined our friends on the patio, Krista was lifting a cardboard box onto the table.

"Before you go in, everyone, take one of these." She was very authoritative suddenly, very in-charge, and I remembered my mom once saying that in times of crisis, we find out what we're really made of.

My mom. I shuddered as I heard her voice again, warning me to stop on the bridge. Had I really just imagined it? Or had she somehow been there?

"Rory? Here."

I blinked. Krista held out a compact black walkie-talkie to me. It had red buttons on the side, and a short, rubber-encased antenna. Beeps and static sounded out as my friends fiddled with their new toys.

"Everyone, make sure you're set to channel one," Krista told us, holding up her walkie and pressing one of the side buttons to show us how to change it. "These have a really good range, so we should be able to stay in touch no matter where we are on the island."

"And modern technology finally gets its hold on Juniper Landing," Kevin said with a grin.

I wasn't even going to touch the irony of that.

Suddenly the back door opened and a few of our new visitors streamed out, including Myra Schwartz, who offered me a wave and a smile, which I happily returned. She was looking stronger, the cut on her forehead covered by a gauze bandage.

"Hurricane watch!" she said. "Can you believe it?"

I had no clue what she was talking about, so I shrugged in response. Luckily, she kept walking and headed across the bluff and down the hill with the others.

"Hurricane watch?" Fisher said under his breath.

"That's what the mayor's come up with to explain the lack of cell service. Big storm moving up the coast, taking out power lines and cell towers." Krista rolled her eyes.

"Not bad," Bea said with a thoughtful frown. "Explains the weather, too."

"Let's get in there," Krista said, glancing over her shoulder as the mayor walked into her office. "She sent me to get you over half an hour ago."

We formed a single line, headed down the side of the living room toward the office. People slipped into jackets and gathered up purses and bags, a few gamely checking their phones. I felt a shiver as my eyes met Selma Tse's. She and her brother brushed by us on their way out the door.

"Odd time of year for a hurricane, isn't it?" Selma said to her brother.

"Yes. Very odd," he replied.

They narrowed their eyes at us but moved slowly and surely out into the rain.

"I really don't like those two," Lauren grumbled behind me.

"Join the club."

Krista shoved open the door to the mayor's office and stood back to let us in. Joaquin and I were the first inside. The mayor was busy shoving papers into a canvas bag. She looked up as we entered, startled, and dropped the bag to the ground at her feet.

"Do you knock?" she snapped, going red around the collar.

"Sorry," Joaquin said sarcastically, raising his hands. "Krista said you were losing it, so we came."

"Did she?" The mayor eyed Krista shrewdly.

"Joaquin!" Krista whispered.

I eyed the canvas bag as the others filed into the room behind me. The mayor kicked it farther under her heavy oak desk until it was out of sight. With one tug on her suit jacket, she was back to form. She eyed each of us as we stood in a long line in front of her. Finally, Krista closed the door and joined us, crossing in front of everyone else to come stand by Joaquin and me.

"Where are we with the search for Tristan and Nadia?" the mayor asked.

The wind whipped the tall grasses outside the window as three black crows swooped toward the rocks cawing and cackling wildly. Every soul who had been up at the bridge with us turned to eye Joaquin and me. My heart throbbed inside my temples as I felt that cold finger run down my neck one more time.

Joaquin cleared his throat. "I think we can safely say we've looked everywhere."

A collective breath seemed to be released in the room. Apparently no one wanted us to admit what we'd done. Suddenly one of the crows landed on the porch railing behind the mayor. It turned its head in that awful, robotic way and seemed to focus its glinting black-eyed gaze on me.

"And you haven't found them? How is that possible?" the mayor demanded, slamming a hand down on her desk.

Everyone flinched. Another crow landed next to the first, its wings flapping noisily.

"They must be on the move, ma'am," Fisher said in that deep, authoritative voice of his. "Staying one step ahead of us."

"If anyone could do that, it's Tristan," Kevin put in, picking at his nails.

"I just wish she'd said something to me," Cori said quietly, looking at the floor so that her braids fell forward over her cheeks. The third crow cawed and came to perch next to its friends. "I wish I knew what she was thinking."

"It's a good question," the mayor said, slamming closed a heavy leather ledger atop her desk. The sound startled the birds, and they whooshed away, bleating angrily as they disappeared into the clouds. "What is Tristan *thinking*? What's his endgame?"

I stared at the book beneath her skinny fingers. Suddenly my whole body was on fire with clarity. "I know how we can find out what he's thinking," I said. "Or at least, what he was thinking before he ran."

The mayor's face screwed up in consternation. "How?"

"His journals."

INTO THE WILD

I watch the never-ending line of visitors as they make their way, bleary eyed and clueless, down the hill toward town. The captives have been released, which means each and every one of those fresh, new visitors is now free to roam the island—to roam right into my waiting clutches. How, oh, how will I decide who my next victims will be? It feels good, having the freedom to choose. It won't be long now before the deed is done and I can reap my rewards.

It's not as if the watchdogs can stop me. Not a chance. I'm unstoppable. I've got pure evil on my side.

GUILT

Now that I've touched her, I know everything about her, and still I can't stay away. The feelings I have when I'm with her terrify me. I promised myself I wouldn't let this happen again. Not with a visitor or a Lifer. But Rory is different from anyone who has crossed my path in a hundred years. I know it's bad for me, bad for her, bad for everyone, but I can't stay away. I keep going to the house on Magnolia to keep watch, to just sit and stare with the mere hope of glimpsing her. The pain when I'm not near her, the anticipation of seeing her again, of hearing her voice, of seeing her smile . . . it's unbearable.

I slammed the journal shut and tried to stop the tears

before they spilled over. The last thing I wanted to do was to cry for him, for us, for what I'd thought we were going to be. I turned my face toward the window of his bedroom, pressing my eyes closed as tightly as I could and biting down hard on my lip. I hated him. I hated him for doing this to me, to my family, to everyone he'd known and loved and cared about for centuries.

A knock sounded on the open door. I quickly swiped at the wetness under my eyes and turned around. Joaquin stood framed by the doorway. Strewn around me were dozens of journals, some lying open, some piled in stacks. The coverlet on Tristan's bed was twisted from the many times I'd changed position over the last few hours as the other Lifers had slowly put their books aside and melted away, tired of reading, hungry for dinner, or just plain unconvinced that this plan of mine would come to anything. I'd been alone and brooding for most of the afternoon.

And now Joaquin was looking at me with pity in his eyes.

"I think it's time to take a break."

I pushed myself up against the pillows, sniffling. "I can't," I said shakily, grabbing another book. "There's something in here. I know it. And I can't stop until I find a way to save Darcy and my dad."

"Rory," he said.

"Joaquin," I shot back, glaring at him.

He took a deep breath and crossed his arms over his chest. "There's something I want to show you. Something I've never shown anyone before."

I slammed the latest journal closed. "You're not going to give up, are you?"

"Have I ever?" he asked, cocking one eyebrow. "Come on, I know you're at least a little curious."

I said nothing. Just stared.

"Come on." He let his hands slap down against his legs. "Your eyes are practically crossed. You haven't eaten since this morning, if then. You're not going to help your dad and Darcy any if you can't think straight. Take a little break."

I heaved a sigh. He was right, of course. My brain was foggy, my eyes were dry, and my stomach was one big, empty knot. Back home I was always the one carefully carbo-loading before a big race, getting plenty of rest the night before an exam. I knew what my body could and couldn't handle, and if I was being honest with myself, it couldn't handle much more of this without giving out.

And in a strange way, it was nice to know that he cared about me. Joaquin had never let me down. He cared about me. And that meant something. It meant a lot, actually.

"Fine," I said as I swung my legs over the side of the bed.

"But then we're coming right back here. I'm close to something. I can feel it."

"Don't worry," he said with a slow smile, his hand grazing the small of my back as I slipped by him. "This won't take long."

ESCAPE

"If you're bringing me up here to kill me, I'm going to be really pissed off," I said, pressing one hand on the flimsy wall beside me as the tower above the library swayed in the wind. I swore under my breath as the entire thing leaned to the left. Overhead, the huge, two-ton bell creaked ominously on its hinges.

"Rory, you keep forgetting," Joaquin said from the winding stairs just below me.

"I know, I know. We can't die," I said through my teeth. "But you'd think that would negate this serious need I have to murder you right now."

Joaquin laughed, and even with all the vertigo, the sound warmed my heart. "Just keep going. You're almost there."

I held my breath and climbed the last five rickety steps to the very top of the bell tower. Tall arched windows looked out in every direction over the island, and a two-foot-wide plank walkway circled the opening under the bell, which stretched down the ten stories to the floor of the building far below. My heart pounded from the climb, from the height, and from the whistling wind that seemed to blast through every one of those windows at once. I gripped the brick casing on the nearest opening and braced myself, trying to release the fear.

"What're we doing up here?" I asked finally. I eyed the bronze bell as it swayed, thinking of the last time it had rung.

A quick flutter of guilt flashed in Joaquin's eyes, but then it was gone. He walked to an east-facing window and sat down. "We're taking a break," he said matter-of-factly. "This is where *I* come when I want to get away from everything. Check it out. You can see every bit of the island from up here."

I took a deep breath and looked out the north-facing window next to me. Sure enough I saw the bridge off in the distance, the cliffs from which my Lifer friends had jumped on the night they wanted to prove we couldn't die, and several beams of light bobbing around on the north-east shore. A search party. They were still looking. Always looking.

"Cool, right?" Joaquin said.

"Yeah."

I sat down next to him and our knees touched. I didn't pull away, like I would have a week ago. There was something comforting about being this close to Joaquin. And at the same time something daring. I looked up into his eyes, and he stared straight back into mine until I blushed. Then we both smiled and looked out the nearest window. My knee was on fire. Never in my life had I ever thought I would be so focused on my knee.

"It's the highest point in Juniper Landing." Joaquin leaned toward me, bracing one hand beside my hip and pointing past my shoulder. I felt his arm graze my neck, and his breath tickled my skin. "Look."

I turned my head, my heart pitter-pattering crazily, and spotted the mayor's house. Sure enough, we were higher than its tallest point—the weather vane, which was still pointed south.

"I know it's hard to believe, but this is usually a nice place to live," Joaquin said quietly. "It's all sun and surfing and swimming during the day, then music and partying and hanging out at night. It's peaceful, usually. Zen."

I looked up at him, wanting to believe it. Willing, in that moment, to believe anything he said.

"Just . . . not since you've been here," he said.

I snorted a laugh. "Thanks."

"Don't get me wrong. It's not like I'd go back and have you *not* come here." He shifted and laid his arm lightly across my shoulders. Suddenly I felt a few things acutely. The breeze brushing a lock of hair against my cheek. The warmth of his skin against mine. The grain of the wood planks beneath my fingertips.

"So you're happy that I'm dead?" I joked, trying to lighten the moment.

He caught my hand. He wasn't going to let me make a game of this. "Yeah," he said. "I kind of am."

My heart thumped as he leaned toward me. Alarm bells went off in my head and throughout my body. This was Joaquin. Tristan's best friend. Darcy's former crush. He wasn't really going to—

And then he was. His lips touched mine, and he slipped his hand down my back, pulling me closer to him. I could do nothing but respond to his kiss. Suddenly I *wanted* to do nothing but respond to his kiss. And for minute upon bliss-ful, endless minute, that's exactly what I did.

Until finally, unfortunately, he pulled away.

Joaquin stared into my eyes. I searched his, trying to find

a name for what I was feeling. Trying to understand what this was, what it meant. What the hell were we doing?

Then, ever so slowly, he smiled, and I realized I didn't care. What mattered was that this felt right. It felt good to be with Joaquin, his arm now around my back, his comforting, musky scent enveloping me. I leaned contentedly into the crook of his shoulder.

"Look," he whispered, kissing the top of my head. "You can even see your house from here."

I tilted my head half an inch. Out on the ocean, three surfers in black rash guards bobbed on the choppy whitecaps. I wondered whether they were Liam, Lalani, and Nick, making good on their date with the waves.

"No. There."

Joaquin gently turned my chin, and sure enough, there it was. Past the quaint, rain-slicked shops of downtown and the colorful trim of the Victorian houses on Freesia Lane stood the pretty little yellow house on Magnolia. It was so bright and cheerful against the miles of grayness it seemed as if nothing bad could ever happen under its roof. There were the upper eaves under which my wide bedroom sat, and there was Darcy's window, and there was the house across the street where Tristan used to sit and keep watch for the girl whose heart he was planning to break. The girl he simply couldn't stay away from.

ENDLESS

My pulse stopped racing. I felt as if I'd just tripped and landed in one of the deeper puddles marring the park. The girl he couldn't stay away from.

Suddenly I was on my feet. The journal. He'd said that it was too painful to be gone from my side for even a minute. And the other day, I'd thought I'd seen a light but brushed it off as a trick—as distant lightning in the sky. Could it be that simple?

"What?" Joaquin asked, staring up at me.

"When was the last time anyone searched Magnolia?" I asked.

He lifted his shoulders, the light dying from his eyes. He didn't want to leave this place yet. He wanted to be with me. And he could tell I was about to run. "I don't know. Last night? A couple of days ago? Why?"

"I have an idea," I said, trying to ignore the pang in my heart. Trying to focus on the positive. "I think I know where Tristan is."

THE GRAY HOUSE

"Park here," I said as Joaquin turned Tristan's Range Rover up Magnolia Street. We had borrowed it from the mayor's house because we would need the backseat if we found Tristan and Nadia, and Joaquin's pickup had only the cab. I didn't know whether it was poetic or plain cruel that Tristan would be brought to justice in his own car. Joaquin hit the brakes, and they squealed. "We don't want them to see us coming."

"Good call." Joaquin shoved the gearshift into park. His fingers balled into fists atop his thighs. I knew the feeling. The tension in the air was so tight I felt like if I moved, the whole world would shatter. If I was right, we were about to find Tristan. I had to believe it. My hope was the only thing I had left.

Bea pulled her Jeep up behind us, and her headlights momentarily filled the SUV before she doused them. Night was starting to fall, but with no sign of the sun, evening didn't look much different from day. Everything was just a darker, murkier shade of gray. I glanced in the side mirror as the doors of the Jeep opened with a muted pop. Five hooded figures piled out and flanked our car.

I rolled down my window as Joaquin did the same. Raindrops slipped along the inside of the car door. Fisher, Kevin, and Cori were on my side, Bea and Lauren on Joaquin's.

"You really think he's in there?" Fisher asked, gazing off toward the house in question.

"I refuse to believe it," Lauren said, her lips pinched. "The searches have been so organized. There's no way he could have been hiding right under our noses all this time."

"Not all this time, but maybe in the last day," I said. "At least, that's what I'm hoping."

"Let's get this over with." Kevin cracked every one of his knuckles, one by one.

"My thoughts exactly."

I opened my door, forcing Fisher, Kevin, and Cori to step back. As my feet hit the sidewalk, I saw a tall figure approaching us from the bottom of the hill. For a second I thought it might be Liam, but then he looked up and Pete's pale skin practically glowed from under his hood.

"What're you guys doing?" he asked.

"We're checking the gray house for Tristan," Kevin said, putting his arm around him. "Let's go."

"The more the merrier," Joaquin said flatly.

We moved together down the sidewalk. I kept one eye on the front door as we approached, in case someone tried to make a break for it. We passed by Bea's house—a tall white colonial about five doors up from our target—and could hear Bea's insane charge, Tess, screeching from the fourth-floor window. The sound coiled my shoulders, and I looked at Bea. Her face was a freckled mask underneath her black rain hat, the area under her eyes puffy and dark.

"Don't even say it." She sighed and shoved her hands deep into her pockets, hunching away from Tess's window. We really had to get the dark souls off the island. One more reason to finish this thing.

Suddenly, the door to the house next to the gray one opened, and out stepped Sebastian and Selma. Everyone on the sidewalk froze. As they walked down the front path toward us, their eyes slid over us like scanners, the movement so in synch and unnatural they could have been twin automatons. It was eerie.

"What were you doing in there?" Joaquin asked.

"This is the house we were placed in," Selma said in her thin, high-pitched voice.

"They placed you here?" I blurted. "I didn't know there were any boarding houses on this street."

"There are now," Lauren said under her breath. *Now* meaning *now that we're so overcrowded.*

The two of them glared at me with their light blue eyes. "There are people here who don't trust you, you know," Selma said. "Any of you."

"People who are going to want to know what's really going on," Sebastian added.

Then they turned as one and walked away, side by side, their steps perfectly matched.

"I bet they're going to meet those people right now," Kevin said acerbically. "Get them to start asking questions."

The theory sent a chill right through me. I remembered far too vividly what Tristan had told me about the last angry mob that had formed on Juniper Landing. It wasn't something I wanted to experience firsthand.

"Why has the mayor not wiped their memories yet?" Fisher asked.

"She tried," Joaquin informed us. "They refused to be

alone in a room with her, and she couldn't have Dorn subdue them, because there were other visitors waiting to speak
with her."

"God, I can't take the freaking crowds anymore," Pete
said through his teeth.

"I know," I said, squeezing his arm as the twins turned
the corner at the end of the block. "Especially people like
them."

Bea rocked back and forth from her heels to her toes. "I
just want one thing to go back to normal around here. Just
one thing."

The wind whistled in answer, spraying us sideways with
a torrent of rain. I wiped my face with the back of my wet
sleeve.

"Look, if we can just find Tristan and Nadia, we can have
everything back to normal by the end of the night," I said,
glancing hopefully up at the dripping gutters on the gray
house. "Once we start ushering people again and the sun
comes out, everyone will chill. Even the twins."

Joaquin blew out a breath, his nostrils wide. "Let's get
this over with."

He hurried up the gray house's front walk and tried the
door, the rest of us following close behind. It was unlocked,
as most houses in Juniper Landing were. Slowly he opened
the door and peeked inside. There were no lights on in the

parlor or the dining room, but I could see a soft glow flickering from one of the rooms at the top of the stairs.

My heart skipped. Joaquin lifted one finger to his lips, then ever so carefully stepped inside. I tiptoed in after him, followed by Fisher, then Bea, Lauren, Kevin, Cori, and Pete, who was bringing up the rear. I noticed that he'd left the door open, which was quick thinking. The click of the latch might alert whoever was upstairs.

Tristan. Please, please let it be Tristan.

Joaquin brought his boot down on the first step. It creaked so loud I almost screamed in frustration.

"Stay to the side!" Lauren hissed. "Steps are sturdier at the side."

Joaquin nodded, looking green, and pressed himself up against the peeling wallpaper along the stairway. I held my breath as I crept just behind him, each step an excruciating eternity. My eyes were trained on the front bedroom door. The door to the room where Tristan had spied on me during those days after we'd first arrived—the room where he'd taken me on my first Lifer tour, when I'd tried to kiss him, and he'd broken my heart.

Temporarily. Because he'd felt he had to. Now I wished he'd just left it broken back then. It would have started healing by now.

We'd reached the top of the stairs. Joaquin and I locked

eyes, and I saw the determination in his. Suddenly I felt weak and childish and stupid. This was not about how Tristan had betrayed me. It was about Darcy and Dad and Aaron and Jennifer and the other innocent souls suffering needlessly in the Shadowlands. It was time to get them back.

"Screw this," I said under my breath.

Then I turned and threw open the door, the others right on my heels. The curtains were drawn. The room was lit by two kerosene lanterns and one small candle. The first thing I saw by their uncertain light was Tristan, passed out diagonally across two sleeping bags on the floor. I lost my breath at the sight of him. He was on his back in a black T-shirt, one arm stretched out at his side, the other crooked awkwardly over his chest with a bandage wrapped around his hand. His legs were splayed in dirty, wet jeans. A hank of his blond hair fell across his forehead like a crescent moon.

He was here. He was really here.

And I didn't know what to do. Laugh? Cry? Scream?

Fisher pushed past me into the room. "Tristan!" He thundered, kicking his booted foot.

Tristan groaned and rolled on his side. That was when we saw the blood. It was everywhere. A thick pool of it, dark as oil, spreading out from behind his head. My hands flew to cover my mouth. Cori, meanwhile, crept along the front of the room as if looking for something, keeping her back to the wall.

"Tristan?" Bea gasped, falling to her knees.

She tentatively touched his head, and the color drained from her cheeks. "It's bad, you guys. His whole skull . . . "

She turned away, swallowing hard, then got up and staggered to the window, ripping the curtains aside and heaving for breath.

"Who would do this? Who would come in here and attack him?" I asked.

Then, suddenly, Cori screamed.

"What the—"

"Nadia! It's Nadia!" Cori was pointing at the floor near the back of the room, shaking. "She's not breathing, you guys! I don't think she's breathing."

I grabbed a lantern and rushed over to Cori's side. The first thing I saw were Nadia's black Converse, twisted over each other. My eyes traveled up her skinny legs, her flat torso, up her neck to her face. I gasped and took a step back. Her eyes were open and staring. Not blinking. There was no life in them.

"No, no, no," Joaquin said, joining us. "That's not possible. She's just screwing with us."

He crouched next to Nadia's body and put his fingers to her neck. His brows knit and he moved his fingers. Then he moved them again. His hand trembled. When his gaze flicked up to meet mine, I could tell he didn't want to speak.

"What?" Bea croaked from the far corner, hugging herself. "What, Joaquin?"

"There's no pulse," Joaquin said, surprised. "Cori's right. Nadia's dead."

Cori wailed and buried her face in Fisher's shoulder. Lauren buckled backward, staggering until she collided with the wall, where she sank to the floor, straggly strands of her wet hair snagging on tears in the ancient wallpaper.

"I don't understand," I said. We were supposed to be immortal. That was the deal. "If a Lifer dies, where does their soul go?"

No one answered, because there was no answer. This had never happened before. Not in anyone's memory. Ice-cold fear permeated the room, trembling the air around us, turning eyes wide and jaws slack. Where had Nadia gone? Where would any of us go?

"Please . . . "

Tristan. His eyes were still closed, but his fingertips clawed at the dusty floor, curling in toward his palm. He groaned and my knees buckled. I threw myself onto the worn throw rug next to him, my heart wrenched inside my throat.

"Tristan?"

I put my hand on his shoulder. He felt cold—impossibly cold—and I could feel the muscles quivering beneath his skin.

"Help . . . " he muttered, the words a half wheeze. "Help us."

And then his body went slack.

"We have to get him out of here!" I exclaimed, looking at the frightened faces around me. "We have to get him to the mayor or . . . or a doctor. Something."

"What about Nadia?" Cori cried. "We can't just leave her here."

"I can carry Nadia over my shoulder," Fisher said, his green eyes flat.

"You can?" Cori asked.

"Fireman's lift. She weighs, like, nothing." Then, to prove his point, Fisher walked over and lifted Nadia's limp body, folding her over his shoulder. Cori gasped and started to sob. Nadia's Lifer bracelet dangled from her skinny arm like it wanted to fall.

"I'll help you with Tristan," Bea offered, pushing away from the window and stepping up to Joaquin.

Tristan let out a weak, gurgly moan.

"We have to move," Joaquin said. "We can't let him . . . "

"Die." Lauren spoke for the first time in five minutes. She'd been so quiet I'd forgotten she was there, but now she turned her dark eyes up at me and stared, her arms limp like a rag doll's at her sides. "*Die* is the word you're looking for."

No one spoke. No one breathed. This wasn't something

we were ever supposed to face. I crouched down next to Lauren and took her hand. "It's going to be all right."

"How?" Her voice went childish as her bottom lip trembled. "How is it?"

I swallowed hard and looked to the others for help. Their faces were blank. A terrified blank. "I don't know, but the sooner we get them back to the mayor, the sooner we can figure it out. Come on."

I gripped Lauren's upper arm and helped her up from the floor. Then Joaquin slid his hands under Tristan's arms and lifted, letting Tristan's head loll back against his chest, where it left a smear of blood. Bea grabbed beneath his calves, and Lauren, Cori, and I led the way out the door, down the stairs, and back into the night. The rain was sharp and driven, like tiny pinpricks against my skin.

This was not what I had imagined when we'd come out on this mission. I'd seen myself indignantly spitting questions at Tristan, him hanging his head in shame. I'd seen us gathering at the bridge to free the innocents from the Shadowlands. When we'd driven down here, I'd thought I knew exactly what I was doing. But now I was more confused than ever.

When we got to Tristan's car, I opened the doors to the back. Bea and Joaquin carefully loaded Tristan onto the seat, laying his head down gingerly.

ENDLESS

"We'll take Nadia in the Jeep," Fisher suggested.

"There's not enough room," Bea said.

"I'll stay with you guys." Kevin climbed into the front of the SUV.

I glanced around—at Kevin, at Joaquin, at Tristan. There was nothing left for me to do except climb into the back with him. The guy who'd betrayed me. The guy who had sent my family to hell. I thought about putting his head on my lap, but it seemed too intimate. So instead, I slammed the door, walked to the other side, and put his feet up awkwardly on my lap, every inch of my body tense enough to snap.

"You okay?" Joaquin asked as everyone else crammed into the Jeep.

I grit my teeth. "Let's just go."

Joaquin got in, and the engine roared to life. He flipped a quick U-turn and started up the hill toward town, the windshield wipers flapping a frantic beat from side to side. I couldn't bear to look at Tristan's face, so instead I stared out the window at the rain.

"It doesn't make any sense. Who would do this?" I said as we drove out onto the town square, the tires sending walls of water flying up on either side of the car. "Who would attack them and leave them for dead? We've all been looking for him. We all want answers."

137

"I don't know," Joaquin said, glancing over his shoulder at Tristan. "I just hope he lives long enough to explain what the hell is going on."

The front tire bumped over a huge pothole, and Tristan groaned.

"Pete," he muttered.

"What?" I said.

Kevin turned in his seat, his dark eyes alarmed. "What did he just say?"

"Pete . . . killed Nadia," Tristan whispered hoarsely.

Joaquin nearly drove over the curb at the north end of town, but he turned the wheel at the last second, sending me slamming into the door. Tristan started to roll off the seat, but I grasped his shirt and steadied him before he could fall.

"Where the hell is Pete?" Kevin demanded.

"He's in the other car!" I said.

"Call them," Joaquin demanded, slamming on his brakes in front of the police station. "Do it now!"

Kevin fumbled for his walkie-talkie. "Lauren! Come in! Is Pete with you? Over."

Joaquin was out of the car and storming toward the Jeep when the answer came.

"No. Why? We thought he was with you. Over."

In the side mirror I saw Joaquin brace his hands on the top of Bea's Jeep and bow his head. I looked at Kevin, my heart sinking into my toes. "Do you remember seeing him in the room at the house?"

He shook his head. "No. Do you?"

I closed my eyes and took a breath, cursing my own stupidity. But how could I have known? There was no way I could have known what we were going to find, let alone that one of our friends was the perpetrator. "He left the door open behind him. I thought he did it to keep from making noise."

"I don't understand," Kevin said. "What the hell is going on?"

Tristan moaned again and turned on his side. The back of his head was a crater of blood and hair and shards of bone. I swallowed back a heaving breath.

"Pete knew what we were going to find in that room," I said grimly. "He left the door open so he could run."

DEATH

"I don't understand. If Pete had already found them, why didn't he just tell us when we bumped into him on Magnolia?" Lauren wondered as we trudged across the sopping grass toward the mayor's house. She had just radioed all the Lifers, telling them to be on the lookout for Pete. "Why did he let us walk in there all clueless?"

"Because clearly he had something to hide," Kevin said. "He had his walkie-talkie. If he wanted to, he could have reported it right away. But instead, he attacked them and left them for dead."

Dead. My brain still couldn't wrap itself around the

fact that we were using that word. Nadia was dead. And Tristan . . .

I looked ahead at Joaquin and Bea. Tristan's body hung limply between them as they shoved through the back door of the house. Cori, Kevin, Lauren, and I hung back while Fisher walked past with Nadia slung over his shoulder. Cori's head was bowed and her shoulders shook. I barely knew her, but I put my arm around her as we followed the others inside. She'd lost her best friend. I knew the sucking void that opened inside you—I was experiencing it right now with Darcy gone—and I wished there was something more I could do.

Every light was on in the kitchen and the wide-open great room beyond it, making for a blinding contrast to the dark night from which we'd come. The clinic had officially closed down now that the last patient had checked out, and the beds had been replaced with the original, beach-chic couches and chairs. The mayor was sitting in the living room in conference with Dorn and Grantz, while Krista stood in the kitchen wearing a yellow dress, making some kind of smoothie with a very loud, very grating blender. She blanched when Joaquin and Bea tromped past her, and the noise died.

"Tristan?"

Her eyes fluttered closed and she leaned forward, her

hips pressing against the kitchen island as her hands flattened against its surface, as if she was clinging to this place, willing herself not to faint.

Fisher trudged across the hardwood floor, his massive boots leaving muddy footprints, and gently deposited Nadia onto the one empty couch. Joaquin and Bea shuffled toward the opposite one, which was occupied by the mayor and Dorn, who both stood up to scuttle out of the way, startled into motion. Neither could take their eyes off Tristan as Joaquin and Bea laid him down. His skin was noticeably paler than it had been at the gray house. When his head fell sideways, exposing his wound, the mayor's mouth set in a grim line.

"What happened?" Dorn asked.

"Nadia's dead," Fisher said in his blunt way. He stepped to the side of the couch and took a wide-legged stance, like a soldier reporting for duty. I was starting to notice that when things got hairy, he reverted to this no-nonsense posture, his own personal defense mechanism.

"What?" Grantz snapped.

"And Tristan's just barely alive," Joaquin added. He shoved his hands through his wet hair and flung his bloodstained jacket onto the floor. It slid across the wood planks and gathered in a heap near the wall. Joaquin braced his hands on the mantel over the fireplace and leaned into it, blowing out a loud breath. Then suddenly he turned on the mayor, his eyes as fierce as a rabid dog's. "Do you want to tell us what the fuck is going on?"

The words hung in the air as we each struggled for breath. In the distance, thunder rumbled. The only other sound in the room was the incessant even ticking of the elegant grandfather clock.

The mayor turned away from us and stood as still as granite.

Chief Grantz was the first to speak, rising slowly from his chair for the first time. "She's *dead*? She can't be dead."

"I was afraid of this," the mayor intoned. Joaquin and I looked at each other.

"What are you talking about?" Lauren asked shakily. She and Kevin still hovered near the front door, the raindrops from their jackets forming a lake around their feet. "Did you know this was going to happen?"

The mayor turned. "I wasn't certain. I was hoping we would be able to find out what was happening—who was to blame—and fix it before it went this far."

"Okay, enough with the vague," Joaquin snapped. "You'd better start explaining right now."

The mayor took a deep, audible breath and stood in front of the fireplace next to Joaquin.

"Here's what I know. Once innocents started being

relegated to the Shadowlands, the balance of the universe began to shift, which is why we saw the island become infested with bugs and death and storms. When we couldn't find the culprit, our only answer was to stop the ushering entirely. It was the only way to guarantee we didn't tilt the balance even further off its axis."

"Of course. We know this," Fisher said, his hands behind his back. "What does it have to do with Nadia?"

The mayor's eyes grew hard. "Well, what you don't know is that your immortality, as it were, is contingent upon your continuing to fulfill your purpose. That is, continuing to help souls find their redemption and move on. So when we stopped ushering souls . . . "

"We made ourselves vulnerable," I said, my mouth dry. I leaned into the back of one of the taller chairs, gripping its brocade fabric for dear life.

"Yes, Miss Thayer," the mayor said. "The longer you refrain from fulfilling your duty, the more . . . expendable you are to the universe."

"So we can die now?" Krista asked shrilly, her voice filling the long, wide room. "Any of us?"

The mayor turned an inappropriately wry eye on her pseudo daughter. "Let's just say I wouldn't go cliff diving anytime soon."

Krista sat down heavily on a kitchen stool. Bea leaned

into the island, her head in her hands. No one else moved.

"Why didn't you tell us?" Bea asked quietly, her eyes wide and trained on Tristan's wound. "Why didn't you warn us?"

The mayor lifted her chin and cleared her throat. "It was a judgment call," she said. "I already had a hundred extra panicked visitors on my hands. I didn't need you panicking as well."

"That wasn't your call to make," Joaquin spat.

"Excuse me?" the mayor asked indignantly.

Joaquin took one step and got right in her face. The mayor was so startled she staggered back, her shoulders colliding with the mantelpiece. The framed photos set up at careful angles along the expanse of the shelf rattled.

"You put us at risk! This? This is *your* fault," Joaquin said, flinging a hand at the couches where Nadia and Tristan lay. "If they'd known, they might have been more careful. Or they might have come back to us sooner. Nadia might still be alive!"

"Back off her, Marquez," Dorn said.

"Let's stop focusing on what we can't change and focus on the problems at hand," the mayor snapped.

"Do we know who did this?"

"Tristan said it was Pete," Bea replied. "He said Pete killed Nadia."

"Pete?" Krista demanded. "Are you serious?"

"What would Pete stand to gain from this?" Chief Grantz asked. "It doesn't make any sense."

"Unless he's the one who's been ushering people and they found out about it," Lauren said.

I felt as if something inside me snapped, like a guitar string plucked hard, the reverberations vibrating throughout my body. "So you think . . . you think Tristan is innocent?"

Joaquin looked me in the eye and my throat closed. If Tristan was innocent, everything changed. If Tristan was innocent . . .

"No," I said out loud. "It can't be. He had the coins. The picture of my family. He . . . he ran."

The day Tristan had fled, the guys had tossed his room and found the one picture I had left of my family in the bottom of his trunk. It had been taken from my house on the night my father had been ushered to the Shadowlands.

"Think about it. In his note he said he was trying to figure out how to get into the Shadowlands to rescue those people. To do that he'd have to spend time near or on the bridge, like you said," Lauren theorized, approaching us from the spot she'd taken against the east wall. "Maybe Tristan and Nadia saw Pete bring Darcy and Asha to the bridge last night. Maybe they were going to tell us, so he tracked them down and—"

"Found a way to stop them," Joaquin finished, staring at Tristan.

I deflated, sinking in to one of the armchairs. For the last few days I had been focusing so much of my energy on hating Tristan, on what I would do and say to him if I ever saw him again, on making myself *not* love him anymore. The idea that he might be innocent . . . I couldn't process it. I leaned forward, elbows to knees, and gasped for air, trying to get a hold of myself.

"We have to bring Pete in," the mayor said. "We need to know why he did this. We need to know how to set it right."

"Do you think he's going to die?" Lauren asked tremulously, gripping the back of my chair.

My head snapped up. The mayor crossed to Tristan— the boy who acted as her son—and knelt next to him. She checked his wound and grasped his wrist between her thumb and fingers. With a gentle touch, she smoothed his blond hair away from his forehead, where the rain and perspiration had plastered it down. It was a perfectly motherly gesture, and until that moment, I wouldn't have believed she had it in her.

Please let him be okay, I thought. *Please, please, please.*

Even as I thought it, I could feel Joaquin watching me, and it took every ounce of self-control to not look him in the eye. I didn't know what he would see there, but I was sure he wouldn't like it.

"His pulse is strong. We need to move him to a bed,

sterilize the wound. Get him some fluids." The mayor stood up and pressed her lips together. Whatever she was feeling, she was keeping it bottled up as tightly as possible. "With any luck, he'll be okay."

Suddenly our walkie-talkies crackled to life. "Bea? Come in, Bea?" Ursula's voice crackled through the speakers. "Pete was spotted in the town square just now. We tried to stop him, but he got away. He was headed for the docks. Over."

I was out of my seat and headed for the door before the last zap of static had faded away.

"Rory, wait—" Joaquin started, but I cut him off.

"No more waiting," I said, already moving toward the door. "I'm going to find Pete, and I'm going to end this before anyone else gets hurt."

Joaquin and Fisher exchanged a look. "We're coming with you," Joaquin said.

"No," I said, whipping the door open. I was hit by a blast of cold air to the face. "I want to do this on my own."

"No way." Bea came up behind Fisher and Kevin, pulling her hat on over her hair. "As of now, no one goes anywhere alone anymore."

I swallowed hard. The girl had a point. After all, we could die now.

"Fine. But when we find him, I get to interrogate him," I said through my teeth.

Joaquin flipped his hood up. "So where do we start? His place? The Swan?"

"You guys?" Cori cleared her throat meekly. Her face was still streaked with tears, but her chin was set in grim determination. I could only imagine what she was going through, losing one of her best friends and finding out that the other was responsible. The very fact that she was able to stand right now made her worthy of awe. "I think I know where he's going."

I glanced around at the others and saw they were just as impressed as I was. I reached for Cori's hand.

"Show us the way."

TOO LATE

"The Bait and Tackle?" Bea asked as the five of us huddled under a battered and torn awning at the north end of the docks. We were standing across the boardwalk from the business in question. "You think he's in there?"

"I can't imagine anyone would dare go in there," I said with a shiver.

The Bait & Tackle was a square, gray-shingled building built into the center of a wide plank dock that stretched out over the bay. The roof was concave on one side, and the whole thing listed to the left so far I was surprised it hadn't already toppled over. The hand-painted BAIT & TACKLE sign was cracked in the middle, right over the ampersand, and hung in a V shape over the front door.

"He started hanging out there late at night a while ago," Cori said with a sniffle, a relentless stream of water pouring off the gutter and onto the shoulder of her black rain jacket. "Tommy told him he couldn't spin in the house anymore, so he snuck a bunch of equipment out here to keep practicing. Nadia and I are the only people he told."

"He hid a DJ deck inside a bait-and-tackle shop because his fake dad wouldn't let him keep it at home?" I asked dubiously.

Fisher sighed. "Tommy runs this place. He's doesn't really keep track of anything. I bet he hasn't even noticed it."

"Pete keeps his stuff covered with a tarp in the back of the stock room," Cori said, her teeth chattering. "So are we going to get him or not?"

Joaquin nodded and stepped out from under the awning. "Fish, you, Bea, and Cori get the front door. Rory and I will go around the back. If he's there, we'll draw him out. He might bolt around front, so keep your eyes peeled."

"Sounds like a plan."

We moved away from the shingled wall, our feet slapping through the shallow puddles that had gathered on the boardwalk's weathered planks. There was one creaky light hanging from a curved metal post in front of the Bait &

Tackle's front door. It swung like a metronome in the wind, illuminating the words on the sign over the door one by one. BAIT. TACKLE. BAIT. TACKLE. BAIT. TACKLE.

We reached the front door. Fisher and Cori stood off to one side, Bea on the other. Joaquin gave me a nod, and we crept around the short south-facing wall of the building, ducking beneath one window that had the blind drawn anyway and paused at the back. The dock stretched out so far over the water I could barely make out the end of it in the storm. Rod holders were screwed to every other pylon so that fishermen could rest their fishing rods while they spent the day hanging out and hoping for a catch. In the distance, I saw a rocky jetty in the bay parallel to the dock, the churned-up waters of the usually placid surface smashing against the stones.

Joaquin stepped up and pounded on the back door. "Pete!" he shouted. "We know you're in there. Come out and we promise you won't get—"

Suddenly the door burst open, swinging outward and hitting Joaquin square in the face. Pete darted out and ran right past me, vaulting over the guardrail on the dock and dropping onto the sand below. Joaquin fell backward, his head knocking against the wood planks. He was out cold. I hesitated a split second, torn between chasing Pete and making sure Joaquin was all right.

"Sonofabitch!" I shouted in frustration.

Then I sprinted as fast as I could along the side of the building, blowing right by Fisher, Bea, and Cori.

"What the hell happened?" Bea shouted.

"Check on Joaquin!" I blurted back. I tore around the corner and up the boardwalk. The stairs down to the beach were yards away, and Pete had a lead on me as he raced along the sand, but in seconds he would hit the jetty. With any luck, he would try to scramble over it, which would be next to impossible with the rocks slicked down by rain and algae. Hopefully it would help me make up time.

Heart pumping, I ran as fast as I could, trying not to think about Joaquin and whether he was okay. Trying not to think about Tristan or Nadia or Darcy or my dad. I had to run the race of my life. Everyone's existence depended on it.

Down on the sand, Pete came to the side of the rocky jetty. He looked back at me, his eyes wild, and started to climb. Finally I reached the stairs down to the beach. I took the turn at a sprint, and my feet nearly went out from under me, so I jumped down to the sand, vaulting past the eight or ten steps. I landed in a crouch, but thanks to the soft, wet ground, the impact was hardly jarring. From the corner of my eye, I saw Fisher running toward us.

Pete was climbing the rocky slope. His foot slipped and his knee went down hard. I climbed after him, gritting my teeth as my sneakers squeaked against the jagged rocks. Sweat prickled down my back, mixing with the relentless rain.

"Fisher! See if you can get down on the other side!" I shouted. "Cut him off!"

"On it!"

Fisher ran ahead, then disappeared from sight. In seconds I was so close to Pete I could make out the pattern of the treads on the bottom of his shoes. Then he jumped to his feet and started carefully across the expanse of the jetty. Suddenly he froze in his tracks.

"Nowhere to go, dude!" I heard Fisher shout. "Give it up."

"Yes," I said under my breath. We had Pete trapped. I climbed to my feet. He turned around, took one look at me, and started to run—toward the ocean.

"What the—"

I took off after him. The terrain was uneven, wet, and pocked with puddles. Dead jellyfish clung to one angled rock, their bulbous bodies torn and limp. I slipped once and my hands came down atop a pile of broken crab shells, pincers, and legs. I gritted my teeth and pushed myself up again. Somehow, I was still gaining on Pete, but it no longer mattered. He'd reached the end of the jetty. His back was to me, and his shoulders rose and fell as he heaved in breath after breath.

"There's nowhere to go!" I shouted. "You can't hide from us forever."

He turned around, his knees like jelly, and looked me in the eye. "I can hide from you long enough."

I blinked. "Long enough for what?"

"For me to get what I want," he said, turning his palms out. His eyes flicked past me, and I turned my head just enough to see Fisher clambering up the rocks nearby. "Listen, Rory. In case something happens, I want you to know, it wasn't my idea."

"What?" I asked, my heart pounding anew. "What wasn't your idea?"

"To take your family," he said quietly. "Or to pin it on you. I was just the muscle."

My brain felt about as steady as the roiling waves behind him. "I don't understand. You're saying you were involved? With Tristan and Nadia? With the ushering?"

He shook his head. "It wasn't them. It was never them."

My head went weightless, everything I had believed, obliterated in one breath. If it wasn't Tristan and Nadia, then who the hell was it? How had they done it? Where had they gotten the tainted coins, and why had they set up Tristan to take the fall?

"Who?" I demanded as Fisher approached me from behind. "Who are you working with?"

"Don't do anything stupid, Pete," he said, his voice rumbling like thunder. "You know better than anyone that we're not immortal. Not anymore."

Pete chuckled. "That's a chance I'm gonna have to take."

Then he took a step back and turned.

"No!" I screeched.

But it was too late. Pete launched himself off the jetty and disappeared beneath the ink-black waves.

HERE AND NOW

Tristan's chest rose and fell under the crisp blue sheets folded across his body. After we'd left the night before, the mayor called in Teresa Malone, a Lifer who had been a nurse in the other world, and it seemed as if she'd taken good care of him. His head was now wrapped in white gauze and positioned flat against a slim pillow, his arms straight down against his sides. I stood next to his bed while the wind whipped outside, pelting the windowpanes with a smattering of fat, relentless raindrops.

It was Friday morning. Thirty-six hours since my sister had been taken and almost eight hours since Fisher dove into the water after Pete and came back empty-handed. Pete had disappeared. He'd either drowned or somehow managed to get away. I hoped like hell he was still out there somewhere, because if he was dead, we'd never get our answers. If he was dead, all was lost.

Dorn was supposed to radio everyone if and when Pete was found, and I'd been waiting on pins and needles throughout the night. Until, that is, I'd finally passed out from utter exhaustion in the bed next to Krista's. When we'd woken this morning, we found two brand-new, shiny gold coins on her nightstand. With Pete on the run, did that mean they were clean? Was it safe to start ushering people again?

The only thing I knew for sure was that we needed to find Pete. He was the only one who would know how to save my family. I checked my walkie-talkie to make sure it was on, and of course it was. Radio silence had become my enemy.

I turned the volume up, just in case, and sat forward, staring at the well-worn leather Lifer bracelet clinging to Tristan's thick wrist. I looked at his profile, his normally tanned cheeks seeming sunken and waxy. He moaned softly, and I wondered if he was dreaming of when Pete had attacked him. Had he seen who was working with him?

I pulled the desk chair over and sat next to Tristan's bed. My hand twitched to take his, but I hesitated, suddenly confused. Tristan was innocent, wasn't he? He was just a victim. Like Darcy, like Dad, like Aaron. And if it could somehow help . . . tether him to the here and now . . . I had to try.

Placing my hand over his, I looked at his face. His skin was warm. That had to be a good sign. Especially after how cold he had felt yesterday. He was improving. Tears welled in my eyes.

"Tristan?" I said quietly. "It's me, Rory. I don't know if you can hear me, but if you can . . . we're here. We're here for you, and we want you to get better."

My voice cracked and I took a breath. "I'm so sorry I thought you were guilty. I should have known. I should have believed. . . . I was just so upset about my dad and now Darcy. . . . " I paused, hearing myself, and cleared my throat. Was I really sitting here trying to make excuses to a guy in a coma? "I'm sorry," I said. "I'm just so sorry."

"Sorry for what?"

My head popped up. Joaquin stood, perfectly framed by the bedroom doorway, wearing a blue-and-gray baseball T-shirt and jeans. Even with the purple bruise in the center of his forehead from when he'd been knocked out earlier, he looked, in a word, gorgeous. And also concerned.

"Nothing."

I slid my hand away from Tristan's, across the sheet, and

into my lap. I lifted my eyes to meet Joaquin's. "Just that I thought he was guilty."

"Everyone did, at some point or another," Joaquin said. He stepped into the room and hovered on the other side of the bed. "How is he?"

"The same. Teresa from the bike shop was with him through the night, and he hasn't woken up."

I shrugged feebly as more raindrops pelted the window behind me. The wind whistled through the gutters and eaves. As the silence between us went on, I started to sweat. Yesterday I had kissed this guy. I had wanted nothing more than to be with him. To let him help me forget the rest of this stupid universe existed.

"Rory . . . " Joaquin said.

I looked him in the eye. "What're we going to do, Joaquin?" I said simply, without thinking.

His shoulders dropped half an inch. It might have been imperceptible if I wasn't so totally in tune with his every movement.

"I have no idea."

Suddenly our walkie-talkies crackled to life. "Rory? Come in, Rory. It's Dorn. Over."

My breath caught, and I fumbled the radio off my waistband, pressing down firmly on the talk button. "What is it? Did you find him?"

There was a beat of silence. A beat too long. "I . . . well, we're not sure yet. Over."

I looked up at Joaquin, and I could feel our panic rising together. He lifted his walkie-talkie to his lips, his eyes never leaving mine. "What the hell does that mean?"

Dorn sighed. "A body just washed up on the beach."

THE BODY

"It's not Pete," Krista said, tears coursing down her cheeks as she intercepted Joaquin and me on the boardwalk outside the Thirsty Swan. Dozens of visitors had gathered at the railing, while Dorn, Grantz, and the mayor stood around the body near the shoreline, blocking it from view. The Tse twins were right at the center of the crowd, their eerie blue eyes focused on the beach, their thin lips screwed into scowls. Liam and Lalani stood off to the side, holding paper cups of coffee that they seemed to have forgotten in the tragedy. Ray Wagner leaned into the railing, the toes of his boots squeaking against the boards as he craned his neck for a better look. "It's . . . it's Cori, you guys." Krista sniffed. "She's dead."

"What?" I blurted.

"No," Joaquin said, the color draining from his face. "No. It can't be."

Fisher and Kevin jogged past us down the stairs with a stretcher, their feet sinking into the wet bay-beach sand with every step. Dorn stepped aside to let them through, and for the first time I really saw her. Cori was facedown in the sand, her curly hair matted by the rain, her sweatshirt and jeans pillowing around her in wet folds. Someone in the crowd gasped as Fisher and Dorn rolled her over onto her back. Her face was completely destroyed on one side, the skin torn away to expose the bone. One of her eyes was missing. I turned into Joaquin's shoulder, squeezing my eyes closed, and he held me tightly.

Cori had always been nice to me. Or tried to be, with Nadia breathing down her neck, hating me as fiercely as she could and trying to get her best friend to do the same. She was so sweet, so meek, so innocent. Why had this happened to her? Why was any of this happening? I had just been with her last night. I had just started to respect her, started to get to know her the tiniest bit. And now she was gone.

"I think I'm gonna be sick," Krista said. "Why would Pete do this to her? They were best friends. Them and Nadia . . . It makes no sense."

"Do they think it was definitely Pete?" I asked.

"I don't know. I've only overheard a few things," Krista said, wiping under her nose with the back of her hand. "I didn't want to go over there."

"I will," Joaquin said. His voice cracked, and he cleared his throat. "We should find out what they know."

"I'll come with." I stepped shakily out of his grasp, pushing my hands into my coat pockets. "Are you gonna be okay?" I asked Krista.

She stared blankly past me. "Do you think he killed her? Do you think he did this because she told you guys where he'd be?"

Joaquin and I exchanged a look. "I hope not. But if he did, that means he's still out there," Joaquin said. "That means we can bring him in."

"Right. And that's a good thing," Krista said uncertainly.

"It's a very good thing," I said, squeezing her arm. It meant we could still get the answers we needed. It meant we could make him pay for what he'd done. To my family, to Aaron, to Jennifer, to Nadia, and now, possibly, to Cori.

"I guess I'll go back to work," Krista said quietly. "Let me know if you find out anything."

"We will," Joaquin said.

Someone had laid a white sheet over Cori's body, and she'd been lifted onto the stretcher. Joaquin and I took the steps down to the beach, and Liam broke away from Lalani to follow us. Fisher gave us a stone-faced nod as he and Kevin hefted the stretcher up the stairs. We joined the mayor, Chief Grantz, and Dorn on the sand. The impression left by Cori's body had already filled up with water and disappeared. It was as if she'd never been there.

"What the hell happened?" Joaquin asked under his breath.

I cast a wary glance at the onlookers. A few of them were starting to disperse now that the body was gone, meandering off toward the Swan or toward town. The twins kept their position, however, each gripping the guardrail with their right hand. Ray Wagner, much to my disgust, was eagerly following Fisher and Kevin as they carried Cori up the hill.

"We don't know," Dorn said, putting his hands on his hips. "She wasn't attacked like Tristan."

"But her face . . . " I said.

"Could be from a fall into the water, or the waves might have knocked her against the rocks." Dorn shook his head. "She never was the strongest swimmer. It could be a simple drowning."

"Except for the fact that she's only the second Lifer ever to perish," the mayor said, seething.

"Can you check her lungs?" Liam asked.

"What?" the mayor snapped.

Unperturbed, Liam lifted one shoulder. "If there's a lot of water in her lungs, that means she inhaled it and drowned. If there's not, that means she was dead before she hit the water. Which would mean . . . you know . . . "

Murder, I finished silently.

Dorn and Grantz exchanged an impressed look. "We'll see what we can do."

"This is a nightmare. Why is this still happening?" the mayor ranted. She wasn't wearing an ounce of makeup, and for the first time since we'd met, her hair wasn't perfectly styled. A few wet pieces clung to her cheek.

"Hold it together, Mayor. We'll figure it out," Dorn said. There was an uncertainty in his tone that chilled me. The mayor was the one solid constant we had in this town. If she lost it, then whatever confidence or hope the rest of us had would be obliterated.

"Will we?" She snapped her eyes wide. "Because we haven't so far. Nadia and Cori are dead. Tristan's in a coma, and now we have another fugitive on our hands. And in case you haven't noticed, the island is about to sink into the damned ocean." She stomped her foot, which only squished further into the thick muck at our feet.

Joaquin turned to the mayor. "We'll find Pete. He doesn't know the island the way Tristan does."

The mayor's jaw was taut. She seemed to have stopped breathing. "You'd better," she said. "Because I'm not sure how much longer we can go on like this."

"What're you saying?" Grantz asked, his face slack.

She turned slowly to look at him. "I'm saying that if we don't find a way to reverse whatever's going on around here, we could be looking at the end of Juniper Landing as we know it."

No one spoke. The rain began to fall harder, the sharp droplets ricocheting off our shoulders and stinging my face. My hand automatically found Joaquin's, and he held it firmly between us.

"Get your search parties out there and find Pete," the mayor growled.

As she stormed up the beach, Joaquin called after her. "What about the funeral? For Nadia? It's supposed to be today."

The mayor sighed and cursed under her breath. "The funeral goes on as planned," she said. "But you and your friends are going to need to dig another grave."

She cast one last look at the spot where Cori's body had lain, then made her way purposefully up the beach. The twins watched her go, following her progress with their eerie eyes.

"The end of the world, huh?" Liam said. "That's something

I never thought I'd see." Then he loped off to rejoin Lalani, taking her hand as they walked slowly up the boardwalk.

Grantz was already on his walkie-talkie, ordering the search parties to the police station. Once the mayor had disappeared around the corner, the twins turned around again, looked me dead in the eye, and smirked. My grip on Joaquin's hand tightened.

"What is it?" he asked.

"Why does it seem like they're enjoying this?" I said, lifting my chin toward the twins.

Joaquin turned to look at them. Neither one of them flinched. If anything, their smiles widened.

"Does anyone know whose charges they are?" he asked quietly.

"No one's mentioned it," I said. "But it's gotten hard to keep track lately."

"See what you can find out." Together we turned toward the stairs. "There's something off about those two. The last thing we need around here is another enemy."

"Okay. I'll ask around," I promised.

When we reached the boardwalk, the twins were still watching. They were the only visitors left, standing at the guardrail in the driving rain.

"I'll see you at the mayor's at ten," Joaquin said, releasing my hand.

For a second I thought he was going to lean in and kiss me good-bye. Part of me hoped he would, and another part wasn't sure how I'd react if he did. But Joaquin simply took a step back and headed down the alleyway toward his apartment.

My hands were shaking. I had to figure out how I was going to handle Tristan being back. If he woke up—when he woke up—I was going to have to make a decision. Did I forgive him for bailing without explanation? Could we move past it? Or should I be with Joaquin, the one person who, so far, had never let me down?

I hadn't taken two steps when the twins appeared on either side of me. My blood curdled and I hugged my arms tightly. Being surrounded by the Tse twins was so not what I needed right now.

"Lost another one of your own, huh?" Sebastian asked.

"What do you mean by that?" I snapped.

"A local," Selma replied. "One of your own."

"Oh." I blinked, wondering how they knew about Nadia. But I supposed this was a small town. News spread. "Yes. We did. But she wasn't just a local. She was a . . . a friend." Or at least a potential friend. "She deserves a little respect."

I quickened my steps, but they matched their pace to mine. Selma's gaze bored into my cheek and I ducked my head, wishing I could turtle into my coat and disappear.

"You should probably get used to it," Sebastian said, a teasing lilt to his voice.

I stopped in my tracks and turned on him. "What? Why? What do you know?"

He raised his hands in a gesture of surrender. "Nothing. Just with this *storm* coming and being on an island . . . there are usually a lot of casualties."

I narrowed my eyes at him as his sister slunk along behind me until she was standing at his side.

"You sure are defensive," she said. "Anything you want to tell us?"

"Yeah," I said through my teeth. "Stay the hell away from me."

I turned to stalk away, but my foot caught on the seam between the boardwalk and the asphalt sidewalk and I tripped. Sebastian's hand shot out to catch me, and the second his fingers touched my arm, my head filled with visions of his life. His death.

Sebastian in a crib lying head to toe with his sister. Sebastian as a boy in a black-and-white school uniform, tormenting a smaller kid. Sebastian scoring a winning goal in a soccer game, then spitting at the feet of his opponent. Sebastian curled up on the floor in the back of a dark closet while his parents screamed at each other. Sebastian and his sister shouting at a rally, hoisting picket signs over their heads. Sebastian and Selma being mugged on a dark street. Sebastian fighting back. A shot going off. Sebastian watching his sister die before being shot himself.

I ripped my arm out of his grip and turned away from them, my eyes filling with tears. He'd died an awful death, watching his sister take her last breaths. But almost more overwhelming were the images of his life. The pain he'd been through, the pain he'd caused. It had been a short existence, but one full of hurt and confusion, anger and fear.

"Wow. Way to say thank you," he spat.

I turned to look at him, water streaming down our faces. My jaw clenched. "Thanks."

Then I turned and started up the hill as fast as I could go. At least now I had half an answer to Joaquin's question. Sebastian was my charge, and one thing was certain—as soon as we set things right around here, he was the first person I was ushering off this island.

THE FUNERAL

I kept my head down as we walked two by two, following the matching caskets down the hill. The service had been brief and cold, as if everyone here had forgotten what wakes and services were actually for—sharing fond memories of the deceased and honoring their lives. The mayor had said a few words in her living room, where the roughly hewn caskets had sat closed on the floor, surrounded by fake flowers, since every real bloom on the island had long since wilted, grown moldy, and died. No one else had volunteered to say a word. But as the caskets were lifted and the crowd parted to form a makeshift aisle down the center of the room, I had suddenly started crying, and I hadn't been able to stop since.

I cried for Cori. I cried for Nadia. I cried over the fact that they had both walked around this island with the same confidence everyone else had—that nothing truly bad could ever happen to them again—until it did. I cried for my dad and Darcy and Aaron. And I cried for my mom, whose funeral was the last one I'd attended on Earth. The moment I let myself open that door, the memories crashed over me like the waves at high tide. The pain was as fresh as if she'd taken her last breath just yesterday.

I thought of the way Darcy had held it together so perfectly, her posture like a prima ballerina's, her smiles so gracious and polite as she'd received the guests, until she'd stepped up to my mother's open coffin and let out an awful wail. I thought of how my father had gotten up from his chair to say his eulogy, but fallen right to one knee, where he'd stayed for at least five minutes until my uncle Morris finally helped him up. I thought of how I'd reached out to hold her hand inside her coffin and stared at her overly made-up face, just willing her to wake up and smile. Wake up and tell me this was just a dream.

Wake up, wake up, wake up, I'd repeated silently, desperately. *Please, Mommy. Please wake up.*

That was the memory that truly caught me now, closed my throat, and made me buckle at the waist.

173

Please, Mommy. Please wake up.

I wished for the thousandth time that I could talk to her, if only for a second. Now I needed her more than ever. I needed her to tell me what to do. I needed her to tell me everything was going to be okay. And I needed Darcy, too. And my father. It wasn't fair that I was alone here. It just wasn't fair.

"Rory?"

I looked up into Joaquin's eyes. I hadn't even noticed that we'd stopped.

"Are you all right?" he asked me.

I shook my head, glancing past the other raincoats and umbrellas at the caskets, which now lay on the grass next to the open graves. The caskets were made of raw birch, the bright yellow grain the only warm spot in the world around us. There was no graveyard in Juniper Landing, of course, and we had decided to bury them near the trees on the lower of the two bluffs at the south end of the island. This was one of the flattest bits of terrain, and a beautiful spot with a view looking over the town to the east and the ocean to the south. From what I had heard, it had taken Fisher, Dorn, and Kevin over an hour to dig each hole because the earth was so saturated it kept collapsing in on itself. Now everyone waited for the caskets to be lowered. For this whole sorry episode to be over.

"I'm fine," I said, shoving my balled-up hand under my nose. "Shouldn't you be . . . over there?"

As one of the sixteen pallbearers, Joaquin was supposed to be helping to place the caskets into the ground.

"Yeah." A pained expression passed over his face, and he held tight to my elbow. "I just wanted to check on you."

"Thanks," I said, and meant it.

I glanced around as I tried to catch my breath. Surrounding the caskets and the graves were dozens of black-clad Lifers, passing tissues, their heads bowed. But beyond them, a small crowd had started to gather. Curious visitors. And I felt a sharp stab of resentment at their presence.

This was a private moment, not a tourist attraction. Even Ray Wagner and Jack Lancet were there. They whispered to each other, their heads bent close. When Wagner caught me watching, he lifted his hand in a jaunty wave. He was enjoying this.

"I think we should get this over with," I said tersely.

Joaquin nodded and got back to the business at hand. He and the other pallbearers—Liam, Kevin, and Fisher among them—lifted Nadia's casket by its plain silver handles and ever so carefully lowered it into the ground, falling to their knees as they gritted their teeth under the strain. When the wood finally hit the dirt floor of the ditch, Lauren let out a choking sob and buried her face in Bea's jacket. Then they lowered Cori's casket into the ground as well, and the mayor stepped up to the top of the graves.

"Today we lay to rest two good friends. Let us never forget what their lives meant to us. What their deaths mean to us."

She crouched down, picked up a glob of muddy dirt, and threw it atop Nadia's casket, then did the same for Cori's. The rest of the Lifers formed a jagged, circuitous line, and each of them followed suit, littering the wood with mud. As I edged forward, I glanced across at the visitors and was startled by a few hostile stares, a few suspicious glances, some furtive whispers. They were talking about us. Talking as if they suspected us of something. But what? We were simply laying two people to rest.

When it was finally my turn, I set aside my unease and scooped up a small chunk of mud. I looked down at a dark brown knot in the lid of Nadia's casket and let the dirt drop and plop from my fingers to cover it.

"Good-bye, Nadia."

I stepped to the next casket.

"I'm so sorry, Cori. I wish I had stopped him. I'm so sorry."

I dropped the mud on her casket, tears coursing silently down my face. Then there was nothing left to do but move on.

Joaquin was waiting for me a few feet away, a black umbrella overhead. "Do you want to get something to eat?"

"No," I replied, kicking at a white rock. "I just want to go home." Though what I thought was waiting for me there, other than loneliness and silence, I had no idea.

He put his hand gently on the small of my back, and we moved away from the crowd. We'd barely made it five steps when the sight of the twins stopped me cold. While most of the visitors were keeping a respectful distance from the proceedings, staying near the point where the hill dropped off toward town, the Tse twins were much closer. They'd chosen a spot in the middle of the field, just yards behind the mourners, standing beneath the cover of a wide black umbrella. Their clear eyes stared directly at me, directly *through* me, making my insides curdle. Sebastian was rolling a coin across the back of his hand from finger to finger, a trick I'd never been able to pull off myself.

"I still can't believe he's your charge," Joaquin said under his breath. "How did you not know?"

"I'm as confused as you are," I said. Normally we knew who our charges were the moment they arrived on the island—knew everything about them once we saw them. Then, when they were the next in line to be ushered, we would find out about their deaths, the better to help them resolve their issues. "Maybe it was because they arrived on the ferry? Everything was such a mess that day."

"Maybe," Joaquin mused, narrowing his eyes at them. "Is it just me or does it seem like when it comes to the Tses, nothing's quite what it should be?"

"It's not just you," I replied.

Just then, Sebastian turned slightly, and I saw that the coin he was toying with wasn't silver, but gold—one of the Lifers' ushering coins.

"Joaquin!" I exclaimed, gripping his arm.

His face paled when he saw the coin. Before he could stop me, I'd taken off after the twins, grabbing Sebastian's arm.

"Get off me!" Sebastian snapped, shrugging off my hand.

My teeth clenched. "Where did you get that?"

"It's none of your business, is it?" he replied, quickly pocketing the coin. "Unless you want to try explaining what it is."

He and his sister eyed me and Joaquin shrewdly, their light eyes glinting with malice. I pressed my lips together tightly.

"We didn't think so," Selma said.

Then they turned as one and walked away, their steps perfectly matched.

"What the hell is going on?" Joaquin asked as a stiff wind off the ocean blew my hair across my eyes.

"Pete said he was working with someone. We just assumed it was a Lifer, but what if it's not?" I turned to face him. "What if one of the visitors has something to do with this?"

"But, Rory, it can't be them," Joaquin said. "They didn't get here until the ferry sank. Aaron, Jennifer, your dad . . . they'd been ushered already."

"Unless they didn't get here that day," I replied, my pulse racing. "What if they've been here all along?"

Joaquin shook his head. "What?"

"Think about it," I said, everything coming to me in a rush. "Steven Nell managed to sneak in under everyone's radar. What if the twins got here earlier and were hiding out until the ferry sank? Maybe they used the confusion of that day to come out of the woodwork and start stirring things up with the locals. Cause a distraction so Pete could keep ushering souls."

Joaquin eyed the line of visitors along the ridge. A few of them parted to allow Sebastian and Selma through, then followed the twins toward town, casting suspicious stares over their shoulders at us. It was as if the Tses were gathering forces. As if some of the visitors had become willing minions.

"Why else would they have a coin, Joaquin?" I asked. "Why else would they be asking us these crazy questions as if they already know the answers?"

Just before he dipped below the hill, Sebastian paused and looked back at the weather vane atop the mayor's house. Ever so slowly, his narrowed eyes slid in our direction, sending a creeping chill down my spine. He smirked and was gone. Joaquin's jaw tightened.

"We should take this to the mayor," he said. "I think it's time she had a little chat with the Tses."

DEAD AND BURIED

I stare at the graves long after everyone else has gone. No one has covered them over yet and the piles of mud on the once clean surfaces seem wrong. Everything about this seems wrong. They didn't have to die, but it wasn't my fault. It was theirs. If Nadia had just stayed in hiding like a good little scapegoat, if Cori hadn't interfered, these graves never would have been dug.

I could have ended this without killing anyone, but what's done is done. There's no going back. Soon I'll have everything I want. And that's the only thing that matters.

DISTURBING THE PEACE

I waited in the lobby of the twins' boarding house on Magnolia that afternoon with Krista, Liam, and Bea, while Joaquin, Fisher, Kevin, and Dorn made their way past the staircase to the door of the first-floor room where the twins had been staying. I still couldn't believe they had been placed so close to my house. The very idea of their proximity to it gave me the creeps. But then again, I had been staying with Krista for the last few days anyway, and hopefully, when and if I ever felt comfortable in my house again, the two of them would be long gone.

I glanced nervously at the front door and the weather

raging outside, and hoped we could get through this without a scene. After the funeral earlier, there was a sort of unease between the Lifers and the visitors.

Fisher pounded on the door. It sounded like thunder. Liam startled and even I flinched. Apparently he wasn't as concerned as I was about being discreet. Not that I was surprised. All my friends were on edge with another member of our group gone—someone they'd laughed with, hung out at the cove with, shared secrets with. They wanted answers, they wanted justice, and they wanted the deaths to stop.

"Selma? Sebastian? We need to talk to you," Joaquin said. "Please open the door."

There was no reply. A door on the floor above creaked open, and I could feel whoever it was eavesdropping. Joaquin glanced at Dorn, who'd worn his Juniper Landing Police uniform for the occasion. His police cruiser—the only one in town—idled out on the street.

"Selma and Sebastian Tse?" Dorn said, heaving a sigh. "This is the Juniper Landing Police. Open up."

Several more doors opened overhead. One man actually stepped over to the top of the stairs, his fuzzy bathrobe hanging wide over a T-shirt and boxer shorts. "What's going on down there?" he asked Bea, who was closest to him.

"Nothing." She shrugged casually. "The police just have a few questions for someone. No big deal."

"Selma and Sebastian Tse, we know you're in there," Dorn said, lowering his voice. "Open the door or I'll be forced to break it down."

"That doesn't sound like nothing," the man said, creeping down a few steps but keeping a safe distance.

I gritted my teeth and stared at Krista, who looked pale against the backdrop of the yellowing flowered wallpaper. This was not good. Finally, the door at the end of the hallway opened a crack, and either Sebastian or Selma—it was impossible to tell which—peeked out.

"What do you want?"

"Mr. Tse?" Dorn began.

"That would be *Miss* Tse," Selma corrected him with a sneer.

"My apologies," Dorn said, sounding not a bit sorry. "Would you please step out into the hallway?"

She didn't move. The door didn't move. "Why?"

"Is your brother inside, miss?" he asked, tugging up on his utility belt.

Selma's eyes flicked to his gun in its holster. "Why?" she said again.

"Because we're going to need you both to come with us."

The door ripped open so fast that the guys jumped back, and Krista grabbed my arm. Sebastian stood there, his fists clenched at his sides. He was seething.

"Come with you where?" he demanded. His gaze darted to Joaquin's face, then Fisher's, then Kevin's, as if he was studiously memorizing every detail. "Are we under arrest? We've done nothing wrong."

"We just want to ask you a few questions," Dorn said firmly.

"So ask," Selma said.

Dorn glanced over at us, and at the man in the bathrobe, then toward the stairs leading up, where who knew how many people were listening.

"We'd rather do it over at the station." Dorn reached for Sebastian, and in a blink Sebastian lunged at him, slamming the much bigger Dorn back against the staircase wall behind him. I flinched and Selma screamed. Almost instantly, Dorn got Sebastian in a headlock and wrestled him face-first to the floor. Liam craned his neck past me to get a better look at the action.

"That was a bad idea," Dorn said in Sebastian's ear. "Now you're under arrest for assaulting a police officer." I heard the cuffs click around his wrists without ever seeing Dorn take them off his belt. The guy was good.

"Sebastian!" Selma cried. "Are you okay?"

"Get the girl," Dorn growled at Joaquin as he dragged Sebastian to his feet. His face was red and his cheeks quivered. He was angry, maybe even embarrassed, that Sebastian had gotten the better of him, even for that one second.

More doors opened and a crowd started to gather. Joaquin made a move toward Selma, but she flinched back. I grabbed his arm.

"Let me try," I said.

He raised his hands. "All yours."

I took a deep breath and approached Selma. Without her brother by her side, she looked scared. Angry, but also scared. She eyed me cautiously, and I turned my palms out in an apologetic way.

"Look, if you just come with us willingly, everything will be fine," I said. *As long as you aren't the one who hauled my family off to hell*, I added silently.

"Yeah, right. Your ape of a cop just mauled my brother," she snapped.

"Your brother attacked a police officer," I shot back, frustration niggling at my nerves. "But if you agree to answer our questions, I'm sure they'll let him off with a warning."

Selma leaned out of the apartment doorway when she heard the police car's door slam. Her hand covered her mouth. I could see how much she wanted to be with him, and recalled from my flashes of Sebastian's life the depth of emotion they felt toward each other.

"Do you want to go with your brother, or do you want to stay here?" I asked. "Alone."

"I'll come," she snapped, grabbing her bag from just inside. "You got any lawyers in this town?"

I shot a glance at Bea, Liam, and Krista as Selma stormed out the door. The twins were not about to make anything easy.

"You guys good?" Joaquin asked as Dorn loaded Selma into the backseat of his car next to her brother. Bea, Krista, Liam, and I were supposed to stay behind to search the Tses' room for more coins, or anything else suspicious.

I glanced back at the apartment. "We'll get it done as fast as we—"

Suddenly, a crackle of static cut me off. Grantz's voice boomed through the speakers on our walkie-talkies.

"Be advised, Pete Sweeney has been located. We're transporting him to the station now. Over."

My eyes widened as I looked at Joaquin. "He's alive."

"This is a good thing, right?" Liam said.

I zipped up my jacket. "I'm going over there."

"I'll come with you," Joaquin offered.

"No. No way." Dorn was standing in the doorway now, practically filling up the space. "I need you and Fisher here with me."

"It's okay. I can go by myself," I said.

"No. You can't. Nobody goes anywhere alone anymore, remember?" Joaquin said, briefly cupping my face with his hand. I felt everyone staring at us—at that brief moment of intimacy—and my skin burned.

"I'll go!" Krista and Liam offered at once.

"You," Joaquin said, pointing at Liam. "You go with Rory. Bea and Krista, search the room."

Krista's eyes filled with worry. It was nice to have someone around who cared about me that much. My friends back home were really more casual acquaintances—people I studied with or ran track with. But Krista had become more than that. She'd become like a second sister. Unfortunately, right now all I could think about was getting my real sister back.

Krista looked at Joaquin. "But Rory might need—"

"Just do it, Krista," Joaquin ordered.

Her shoulders slumped. "Fine."

"Come on," I said to Liam. "We're wasting time."

On my way out the door, Joaquin grabbed my wrist and turned me to him. I could feel the excitement, the anticipation, coming off him in waves. "You radio me the second you find out what's going on," he said, glancing at the twins, who sat whispering in the back of the cruiser. "By the end of the night, one of these people is going to talk. We're gonna get them back, Rory."

His energy was contagious, and for the first time in days, hope filled my heart. I nodded. "We're gonna get them back."

TOO LONG

"He's unconscious?" I said, standing in the stiflingly hot and humid hallway outside the prison area in the basement of the police station. Chief Grantz was drenched with rain and smelled of pungent sweat. Heavy bags settled under his eyes like water balloons. His dark blue vinyl JLPD jacket had a long tear up one arm, and mud covered his black boots, soaking the hem of his police-issue pants as well.

"Yep," he said, wiping his face with a rag. "We found him at the foot of the wall at the cove. Looks like he slipped and knocked himself out."

"You could have maybe said that on the walkie-talkie," Liam said.

Grantz shot him a beady-eyed look. The man seemed as if he were one sarcastic remark away from a meltdown. "Teresa's in there with him now, assessing him. You can go in if you want."

I nodded and he opened the door for us. There were two very tiny cells with bars comprising their front walls and the walls between them. Goose bumps popped up on my arms, and I shivered as I moved aside to let Liam in behind me.

Pete was laid out on the cot in the first cell, blankets piled over him. His face was turned to the side, away from us, but I could see most of his cheek, chin, and one ear. He looked fine, just a bit pale. At least his skull was intact.

Why couldn't we just find someone who was conscious for a change?

Teresa, a woman of about forty with short graying hair, knelt next to the cot holding Pete's wrist between her fingers. She looked up as we came in and placed his arm gently down on the bed. My teeth clenched as I tried to fight back my vindictive side—the side that felt that Pete didn't deserve such care when he was the one who had taken Nadia's and Cori's lives, who had rendered Tristan unconscious.

"How is he?" I asked.

Teresa stood up and sighed. "Vitals are fine, but he's out cold. Only time will tell."

"Do you have any idea when he's gonna wake up?" Liam asked, pushing his hands into his pockets.

Teresa opened the cell door with a clang and slipped out. "Unfortunately, no. But it's not as bad as what Tristan suffered. I'd say a few hours maybe? At most a day or two."

A day or two. I thought of my dad and Darcy and squeezed my eyes closed as a wave of despair crashed over me. Every hour, every minute that they were in the Shadowlands was too long.

"You're Liam, right?" Teresa said, lifting her chin. "The mayor told me it was your idea to check Cori's lungs. Good call. I did a rudimentary autopsy, and they were full of salt water. Turned out she did drown."

Liam looked at me. "I guess that's a . . . good thing?"

"It ups the chances that it was an accident," Teresa replied.

"Maybe, but it doesn't prove anything," I said. "Dorn made it sound like everyone knew Cori wasn't a great swimmer. If he shoved her into the water, the way it's been raging lately . . . "

Liam went green and I trailed off. I didn't want to think about it in too much detail, either—the callousness it would take to do something like that, the terror Cori would have felt as she slipped away.

"You could go in and try to wake him up if you want," Teresa suggested, tilting her head toward Pete's bed.

I bristled at the thought. Nothing that I had to say to Pete would make him want to wake up. I was just about to tell her as much when Pete suddenly sighed and turned his head. His eyes were still closed, but I froze, grabbing Liam's arm. Beneath my grip, his whole body went tense.

"Oh my—" Liam said, biting down on his lip.

"Pete?" I asked. "Pete? Are you awake?"

Teresa slipped a tiny flashlight out of her pocket and moved to the bed. She pried open one of Pete's eyes and shined the light in it. He didn't flinch.

"He's still out," she concluded, shrugging at us.

Liam's skin had gone waxy and pale. "I think we should go." He darted for the door like the room was on fire.

"Shouldn't we stay in case he wakes up?" I said.

Liam paused with one hand on the doorknob. "Why? She said it could be days. I say we go up to the mayor's and find out if the Tses are talking."

It was tempting. At least I knew the twins were conscious. I glanced back at Pete, whose eyes stayed stubbornly closed, his chest rising and falling at a normal, calm rhythm.

"I can radio you when he wakes up," Teresa said, laying a comforting hand on my arm. "Go ahead. Neither one of you should be going anyplace alone."

"Okay," I said reluctantly. "Thank you."

Liam shoved through the door. I listened as his footsteps retreated down the long hallway, but I didn't follow. Instead, I waited until Teresa left the cell and closed the door behind her. Pete had ushered my father and my sister and Aaron and Jennifer and all the other innocent people to the Shadowlands. I wasn't going anywhere until I knew for certain that he was locked up good and tight.

Teresa pulled out a big, old-fashioned key and placed it inside the lock. When she turned it and the catch slid into place, it let out a loud, satisfying clunk.

"Where does that go now?" I asked, eyeing the key.

"Back to Chief Grantz," she said. "His is the only key." She smiled in a friendly, knowing way. "You can come with me if you like."

"It's not that I don't trust you. I just—"

"Honey, if I were you right now, I wouldn't trust which way was up," she said, giving my hand a quick squeeze. "This way."

"Thank you," I said, and meant it. It was the first time anyone had made me feel as if my insane emotions were understandable in such simple terms.

I followed her down the long hall, which opened up onto the back of the police station. Together we walked to Grantz's office, and I watched her hand over the key, which he tied to a chain that was attached to his belt. Liam was waiting for me near the front door.

"Good?" Teresa asked, turning to me with a smile.

"Good," I said. "You'll call me when he's awake?"

"The second he starts talking," she assured me. "Don't worry, hon. One way or another, this is gonna be over soon."

I nodded and joined Liam at the door, feeling heavy and hollow at the same time. One way or another. It didn't inspire much confidence.

RABBLE-ROUSERS

"Something really weird happened to me today," Liam said.

We were climbing the hill to the mayor's house through the wind and the rain. Both of us were bent forward against it, like two storm-tossed ships trying to cut through the waves.

"Weirder than usual?" I asked.

He nodded as we reached the top of the bluff. "I was helping Nick up after he got pounded by a wave, and I got this flash. . . . I saw how he and Lalani died."

There was a crack of lightning directly overhead. We ran for the cover of the porch roof at the mayor's house. Heaving for breath, I pushed my hood off my hair and looked at Liam. His face was half lit by the overhead lamps, and he looked, understandably, freaked.

"That means he's your first charge," I told him. "He's the first person you're going to usher. Once we get this mess figured out."

Liam looked at his feet. His Converse were soaked through. "That's what I figured."

"Are you okay?" I reached out to touch his arm, and he flinched, violently, away. I drew my hand back, my heart hammering. "Liam?"

He scoffed at the ground. "Sorry. I just . . . it's been a weird day."

Then he turned and yanked open the door, ripping his jacket off as he barreled inside. I took a deep breath, shaking off the awkwardness, and followed. Joaquin stepped away from the wall where he'd been leaning, and Krista hurried toward me from her post near the office door, where she'd clearly been attempting to eavesdrop.

"Well? How'd it go?" Joaquin asked.

"What did he say?" Krista added.

"He's unconscious," I said flatly, shedding my rain jacket and hanging it on the nearest hook.

"What?" Fisher blurted. He was sitting on the stairs with Bea, who leaned the side of her head against the wall, looking exhausted.

"Teresa thinks it'll only be a few hours," I said, trying to stay positive. "How's it going here?"

Liam had lain down on one of the couches in the living room and was rubbing his face with both hands. Kevin was on the other couch, across the coffee table from him, his arm slung over his eyes. I could hear him snoring lightly. It was an odd time to take a nap—what with our number one suspects being interrogated in the next room—but I could hardly blame them. Every last one of us could have slept for weeks at this point.

"She's still in there with them," Joaquin said, nodding at the office. I could hear voices talking in calm tones from inside. "You should have heard the way they freaked when we brought them here instead of the police station. Those two are not of the wallflower variety."

"Did you find anything at their place?" I asked Bea.

Bea sighed and pushed her curly hair back from her face with both hands. "Nothing. Not even the coin you guys saw. He must have it on him."

"How the hell did he get ahold of a coin?" Krista asked, running her hands up and down her bare arms.

"Maybe he woke up with one next to his bed," Fisher mused. "There's been a lot of random crap happening around here lately. You never know."

We fell silent. I didn't like the idea that the coin was

simply a mistake or a coincidence. I wanted the twins to be part of this. I needed someone—anyone—to blame. Someone to tell me what the hell was going on and how to fix it. I wanted my sister and my dad back so badly it was causing a constant ache in my chest.

"I'm gonna go upstairs and check on Lauren and Tristan." Bea pushed herself up slowly.

Lauren had taken the day shift on Tristan Watch, hanging out by his bedside in case he woke up. She'd taken Nadia's and Cori's deaths—the very fact that we now *could* die—harder than anyone, and was clearly terrified of losing Tristan as well. Somehow, being with him comforted her, as if simply watching his chest rise and fall gave her hope.

Bea had climbed two or three steps when the office door suddenly opened. Fisher stood up. Joaquin pushed away from the wall again. Even Kevin flipped over on the couch, blinking at us with bleary eyes.

"Thank you so much for coming. I hope you enjoy your stay," the mayor said pleasantly, holding the door for the twins to walk through. My heart caught and I glanced at Joaquin as the two of them strolled by us, smiling like content tourists.

"You're letting them go?" Joaquin asked.

"Shh!" the mayor replied curtly.

She opened the front door for them, as well, and waited

with a stiff grin on while they lifted their hands and disappeared into the night. The door closed with a bang, and the mayor pressed her palms together.

"The Tse twins are innocent as pie," she said, her lips pursing sourly around the words. "They are incredibly suspicious people and were career activists in the other world. The current situation on Juniper Landing understandably awoke their inner rabble-rousers, but they have nothing to do with what's been going on here."

"Oh, come on!" Joaquin blurted. "Then where did they get the coin?"

"He claimed he found it outside the general store," the mayor said, casting an accusatory glance around the room. She moved to the window next to the front door to glance out at the stormy sea. "Fortunately I was able to wipe the ferry accident from their memories and alter their perceptions of tonight's activities so that when they go back to the boarding house, they'll have the story of a silly misunderstanding to tell, but that's that." She took in a sharp breath and blew it out. "They should be perfectly happy here for the duration of their stay. What we need to do is figure out how long that will be."

Thunder rumbled in the distance.

"You want us to start ushering again, don't you?" Bea asked quietly.

"If Pete was, indeed, responsible for this mess, I see no reason not to get on with our business now that he's locked up." The mayor's eyes darted from face to face, waiting for someone to contradict her. "Have any of you received new coins today?"

"I have," I said.

"Me too," Kevin called from the living room.

"We all have," Joaquin said, pushing his hands into the pockets of his jeans and looking at his feet.

"Then those coins will be used first, as there's no way Pete could have tampered with them," the mayor said. "We need to start ushering the dark souls and admitted criminals off this island. Right now, we're working on borrowed time. We'll start tonight."

"Tonight?" Krista blurted, glancing out at the sky.

"The sooner the better," the mayor answered.

"But what about the other souls?" I interrupted. "The ones we know should head to the Light? And the children? How will we ever feel comfortable ushering them?"

"We're just going to have to trust that everything will right itself," the mayor said. "And then we'll see."

We'll see. Hopelessness settled in over my shoulders, thick and oozing, like the muddy dirt we'd dropped at Nadia's and Cori's graves.

"I wish Tristan would wake up," Bea said. "Maybe

whoever was working with Pete was with him that night at the gray house."

We looked up the stairs where, aside from the usual rhythm of the rain against the windows, everything was still. There was nothing but shadows, the sliver of light under Tristan's door, the dull crystal on the cut glass light fixture. But I could still see him standing there, his tan skin lit by an inner glow, as he smiled down at me. As he made me feel like I was the only girl he could ever love.

"I'm going up there," I decided, skirting around Fisher.

"Why?" Krista asked.

"I'm going to talk to him," I said, lifting my palms. "They say they can hear you, right? Maybe if he hears my voice . . . I don't know. I'm just going to talk to him."

"I'll come with you," Joaquin offered, his foot hitting the bottom step.

"No."

He froze, and the rest of the world seemed to freeze along with him. "No?"

I couldn't look him in the eye. Not right then. "I want to do this alone. I have to."

"But I—"

"Jay," Bea said. "Let her go. Who knows? Maybe it'll work."

I shot her a grateful smile and didn't wait for him to

answer. Instead I ran up the stairs two at a time and, finding myself in front of Tristan's closed door, took a deep breath.

You can do this, I told myself. *He loves you. He even said so in his note. He never stopped loving you. If there's anyone he'll come back for, it's you.*

With these hopes ringing inside my mind, I pushed open the door. Lauren looked up. She'd been reading aloud to him from a book, seated in the desk chair next to the bed, but fell silent when she saw me. Her short dark hair was back in a plaid headband, and she wore a pink polo shirt, one corner of the collar just starting to fray.

"Any luck?" she asked.

I shook my head. "The Tses don't know anything, and Pete is unconscious."

She slumped back in the chair, the book going slack in her lap. "This is so very bad."

"Mind if I talk to Tristan alone?" I asked.

She glanced at his face, so still it looked like a painting, then sighed. "Sure." As she got up, she reached over to squeeze his hand, then walked out, closing the door behind her. I took the seat she'd just vacated. It was still warm.

"Hey, Tristan," I began, and my voice broke.

I took in a staggered breath, blinking back a fresh wave of tears. Seeing him in this state, motionless and vulnerable, was so very wrong. The Tristan I knew was stronger than any of us, in both body and soul. I remembered, suddenly, the firmness of his arms as he kissed me for the first time. The warmth of his hand as he held tightly to my fingers, swinging our arms between us as we walked from the bridge into town. There had been a time, not that long ago, when there was such an amazing, hopeful, loving lightness in his eyes, and I'd brought it out of him. We were happy.

There was no way I was ready to let that go.

I reached out to take his hand and cupped it with both of mine.

"Tristan," I said firmly, "I want you to know that I'm sorry I didn't believe in you. I know I said that already yesterday, but I am. I am so, so sorry. I hope that you forgive me. No, I *know* that you'll forgive me when you wake up. I know that you'll understand."

Tears fell from my eyes, and I bent forward, resting my forehead atop the back of my own hand. The top of my head hit his side, and I leaned into it, relishing any contact, wishing I could crawl in next to him and hold him close.

The thought that I might never see his eyes again. That I might never feel him hold me again. That I might never touch his lips again . . .

I had to force myself to breathe.

"Tristan, please," I whispered, lifting my head and looking up at his placid face. "Please don't die. Please don't do this to me. I know that what I'm saying is selfish. I know it. I do. But I can't take this anymore. I can't handle losing you on top of everyone else. There are only so many people in this world I love, Tristan, and they're all gone. Every one of them. Except you."

I leaned back, willing him to blink, to gasp, to do anything. Anything to show me that he was still in there, that he could hear me, that he understood.

But there was nothing but the steady rise and fall of his breath, and the ticking of the grandfather clock downstairs.

THE RETURN

"So let's break it down," Kevin said, dropping onto a blanket in the sand next to a roaring, comfortingly warm and dry bonfire. The rain had stopped at three o'clock. Just suddenly stopped after days and days of relentless soaking. It was still drab, gray, and cold with a solid layer of fog overhead, but it was dry, so we'd decided to meet up at the cove for a dinner of sandwiches and chips—which was great, since I couldn't remember the last time I'd eaten—and to figure out our next move. Kevin popped open a can of beer and took a swig, licking the suds from his lips. The skin on his knuckles was dry and cracked, tiny white flakes clinging to his skinny fingers. "Pete is the bad guy. He killed Nadia, and he may have killed Cori."

"Yep," I said, tossing a piece of driftwood into the popping, crackling fire.

"And he has an accomplice, but we have no clue who it is, and he can't tell us who it is, because he's unconscious," Kevin continued.

"Yep."

"Well, this totally sucks."

Kevin chugged the rest of the beer, crushed the can, and reached for another one. I poured coffee from Krista's plaid thermos into a Styrofoam cup, then shuffled through the cool, damp sand and sat on a towel between Krista and Bea.

"I still can't believe we thought it was Tristan," Lauren said, shivering under the gray wool blanket she had arranged over her legs.

"None of us can believe we thought it was Tristan." Kevin tugged his black baseball cap lower over his brown eyes. "But let's not go there right now. I want to talk about Pete. That fucking little backstabber, Pete."

"It doesn't make any sense," Bea said as she reached into a crumpled brown paper bag for a sandwich. "Nadia was one of his best friends and he just kills her? Why?"

"He said if he waited long enough he'd get what he

wanted," I told them, probably for the dozenth time. "So what does he want?"

"Pete? Aside from a lifetime supply of beef jerky and a record deal, I have no clue. He's a pretty simple guy," Fisher said.

"God, I wish he'd wake up," I muttered, checking my walkie-talkie. It's red "on" light gleamed brightly as if laughing at me. I dropped the hem of my jacket over it, annoyed. Bea tore her sandwich in half and handed one side to me.

"I say when he does wake up, we break each of his fingers one by one until he talks," Kevin said, hunching his shoulders toward his ears as he took another loud slurp of beer. "That'll do the trick."

"You wouldn't actually do that, would you?" Liam asked, alarm lighting his handsome face.

"No!" the rest of us answered in unison. To punctuate the message, Fisher flung a scrap of bark at Kevin's head. It bounced harmlessly off the bill of his cap.

"That is *not* the way we do things," Krista snapped, brushing some ash off the sleeve of her white sweatshirt.

"How do you know?" Kevin asked, sitting up straight and pushing the cap up on his forehead to better glare at us. "How do any of us know? It's not like anything's normal around here. Who's to say how we do or don't do things?"

Bea took a deep breath and sighed. For the first time in

days, her red curls were loose around her shoulders, and they danced and shook in the cold ocean breeze. "He does have a point. It is a whole new and not-very-pleasant Juniper Landing."

"But we're not torturing anyone," Joaquin said firmly. "End of discussion."

Suddenly our walkie-talkies buzzed in unison, and there was an awful, piercing peel of feedback, so loud I wouldn't have been surprised if our ears had started to bleed. I grabbed at my radio as Krista ducked her head into her hands dramatically.

"Apologies," Chief Grantz's voice blared through the radios. "My apologies for that. Let all ushers be advised that the mayor has decided the usherings will begin tonight at sundown."

There was no movement other than the endless wild dance of the flames and the meek waves of low tide, lapping at the shoreline behind me. I stared at Joaquin. His jaw clenched as he tossed another twig, then another, then another into the fire.

"The souls on the watch list will be the first to be ushered, as previously stipulated. Please bring your first charge to the bridge once it's dark. Over."

Lauren hugged her knees up under her chin. "Well. So there you go."

"I'm sorry, but I cannot *wait* to get rid of Tess," Bea said, munching on her sandwich. "I'd usher her ass right now if they'd let me."

"Yeah, I won't mind getting rid of Lancet, either," Joaquin said.

"And if I hear Piper ask for Wi-Fi one more time . . . "

Everyone laughed, but it was a short laugh. I stared at the flames, thinking of Ray Wagner's ridiculous taunts, his blackened tongue, his rotting teeth. We were lucky he hadn't tried anything yet. Booting him off the island would be a relief.

But once he'd been ushered, he'd be in the Shadowlands. With Darcy, and my dad, and Aaron. What was it like for them there? Would they have to deal with him, or did they even know where they were, and who else was in there with them? Were they in constant terror, or was it a vast loneliness?

I shivered violently, and my fingers curled into fists at my sides. I had to save them. How was I going to save them?

"Let's just hope none of them go to the Light," Krista said with a shudder. "That would not be good."

I looked at Joaquin. His Adam's apple bobbed as he tore the tiny twigs from a branch. Krista's words hung in the air between us.

"Is this a party or a funeral?"

"Tristan?"

I scrambled to my feet, spraying sand into the fire and over Bea's legs. Tristan walked toward us slowly, his shoulders a bit curled, his chin hanging lower than usual with a square white bandage taped to the back of his head. His blond hair was stringy and two shades darker after going unwashed for days. But he was alive. He was awake. And he was here. After a catatonic second of shock, Krista raced forward and threw herself into his arms.

"You're okay!" she cried.

Tristan hugged her back, first with one arm, then the other. I heard him laugh, and it brought tears to my eyes.

"Apparently I'm gonna live," he said. Krista still had her arms around him, but his eyes met mine over her shoulder. An intense shock of joy shot through my chest and lifted me onto my toes. "Everything's gonna be okay."

They were the words we had all been waiting to hear from the person we'd needed to hear say them, and the mood on the beach exploded. Fisher produced an old-school boom box from the depths of his tent and turned on some base-thumping dance music. Krista whipped out a box of doughnuts from her canvas bag, and Kevin spent the next ten minutes trying to convince us that Boston creams paired perfectly with a lukewarm Bud.

But I had no idea what to do with myself. Everyone else

had mobbed Tristan, laughing and hugging and cheering, while I stood awkwardly in the sand, waiting. The only thing I knew for absolute certain was that I would not approach Tristan. He would come to me. Or he wouldn't. Either way, I wasn't about to make the first move.

Before long, the crowd around Tristan started to break up, and Joaquin was introducing Liam to Tristan. Then, the two of them were alone.

Tristan and Joaquin. Best friends. Brothers. Their conversation shifted from intense to laughing and back again. The sight of the two of them together made me sweat under my dark blue hoodie. Would Joaquin tell him about the kiss? And did it even matter when everything else was so very wrong?

"You gonna be okay there, Killer?" Bea asked me under her breath, handing me a chocolate doughnut.

"I'm fine," I said. "Why wouldn't I be fine?"

She tilted her head dubiously, like she wasn't quite sure I knew the meaning of the word. "Whatever you say." Then she stutter-stepped over to Krista and Lauren, who were dancing together down by the water, trying to drag Liam into the center of their gyrating circle.

"Hey."

When he spoke, so close behind me, it was as if I hadn't heard the sound of his voice in a year. I turned around slowly, and I was looking into Tristan's deep blue eyes.

"I heard about Darcy," he said, his face creased with concern. "I'm so sorry, Rory. Are you all right?"

I trained my eyes on the sand, on the toes of his sneakers. There was a bit of seaweed stuck to the rubber upper, twitching in the breeze.

"No," I said, my voice cracking. "I'm really not."

He reached for me, and I took an instinctive step back. I didn't dare look around. I didn't want to know who might be watching.

"I'm so sorry, Tristan."

"For what?" he asked.

"For Nadia and Cori," I said. "And I'm sorry I didn't believe in you. I'm just so sorry."

"Hey." I felt him moving to touch me again, and I flinched. Tristan's hands fell to his sides.

"But I just can't . . . I can't sit here and pretend that everything's going to be okay," I said, fumbling for the words to express how I was feeling. "How if we just start ushering people, everything will go back to normal. Because it won't. It can't. Not for me and not for the people trapped in the Shadowlands. We can't forget about them, Tristan. We can't pretend like it never happened."

"We won't," he said. "I promise you. We won't forget about them. We'll get your dad and Darcy back."

I glanced around at Fisher and Kevin laughing by the stereo. At Bea, Krista, Lauren, and Liam dancing near the waves. A seagull cawed and dove toward the water. It was the first live bird I'd seen in days. My jaw clenched.

"It feels like we already have," I said.

A tear slipped down my cheek and I quickly, angrily, swiped it away.

"Rory—"

"I'm sorry," I said. "I'm glad you're better, I just . . . Right now I need to be alone. I need some time to think."

And then I did something I never would have thought possible as recently as an hour ago. I turned my back on Tristan and walked away.

IT MATTERS

I was staring at the waves when I saw a flash of color out of the corner of my eye. Joaquin was walking briskly toward the rock wall, snapping up his jacket as he went. I couldn't let him leave without saying something to him. What that would be, I had no idea, but I couldn't let him go.

He was already at the foot of the hill, the rocks slick with leftover rain, when I caught up to him. "Joaquin! Wait up!"

He paused with one hand on a protrusion of gray stone and blew out a sigh. I could practically see him bracing himself to talk to me—the tension in his face and across his back.

214

"We have to talk," I said, planting my feet in the sand in front of him.

"I don't see why," he said, lifting one shoulder. "I saw the way you looked at Tristan when he first walked up. I get it. I'm happy for you."

Never had those words been said in a less enthusiastic tone. He sounded like he was ordering paper over the phone.

"Joaquin—"

He laughed sarcastically.

"Rory, look. I don't want you to get the wrong idea," Joaquin said. "It's not like I'm going to stand here and say it doesn't matter to me. Because it does. Of course it does. If it were anyone else . . . "

He looked off across the beach at Tristan, who was nodding pensively as Kevin went on about something.

"But it's Tristan," I said, my voice full.

When he looked at me again, his brown eyes were full of sadness and longing. "It's Tristan."

My eyes filled with tears, and I could feel him straining not to reach for me. Never had my heart felt so confused and sick and at war with itself. I had spent days hating Tristan, and now, even though I knew Tristan hadn't deserved that hate, even though I knew I loved him, I couldn't imagine letting Joaquin go. I didn't want to lose him.

Finally Joaquin turned toward the rock wall, and the spell

was broken. One tear slipped from my eye, and I swiped it away. Joaquin reached for a handhold.

"Listen, Tristan says that Pete was the only one in the gray house that night. No one else was with him. If that's true, then hopefully the mayor is right. With Pete in prison, we'll be okay."

"Okay . . . " I said slowly, confused by his sudden shift to calm, cool, and collected. All business. "But then what was he talking about when he said it wasn't his idea? When he said he was going to get what he wants?"

"I don't know. Maybe he was just trying to throw you off," Joaquin theorized. "Either way, I'm going to bring Lancet up to the bridge around nine. If you and any of the others want to meet me there . . . it might be good to do it together. Moral support and that kinda crap."

I managed a smile, even though my chest felt bruised. I couldn't believe Joaquin was just walking away from us after everything that had happened. "Okay. I'll tell them."

He nodded and started to climb. His back was to me and he had only one foot planted on firm ground when I spoke again. "Joaquin?"

He turned his face only slightly, so I could see his ear and the corner of his eye. "Yeah?"

"I just want you to know . . . it matters to me, too," I said. "You, I mean. You matter."

He stood there for a second, just letting that sit, and then he climbed away. I stepped back and held my breath for a good long while, wishing it didn't hurt so much to watch him go.

THE BAD-GUY LIST

"What're we doing here, blondie?"

"Just keep moving," I replied.

I glanced past Ray Wagner at Bea, who was busy drag-ging family-slaughterer Tess Crowe out of her Jeep by the light of half a dozen cars' headlights. All our friends except for Kevin—who was keeping watch on the weather vane in town—and Tristan—who was resting—were present. We'd decided that Bea should go first, since she claimed she was going to go insane if she had to spend one more minute in Tess's presence. We stood back and watched as the woman gnashed her teeth and rolled her head around, Bea leading her by the length of rope that tied her wrists together. Jack Lancet slouched near the grille of Joaquin's truck, his bulbous eyes wide, while Piper Malloy paced back and forth in front of Lauren and Fisher, her patent heels gleaming.

At the foot of the bridge, Bea slapped a coin into Tess's hand.

"Happy trails!" she said loudly.

Then she shoved Tess into the wall of mist that surrounded the bridge. I felt a chill as she was engulfed, remembering vividly the horrors that had awaited inside that wall of fog. I half expected her to come tearing right back out of there, but as was normally the case with charges being ushered, she went in the correct direction. After a few seconds, we heard the telltale, louder-than-a-bullhorn sucking sound that indicated whoever was on the bridge had been ushered to their final destination. The stillness that followed felt unnatural, like some unseen hand had hit a giant button, pausing us where we stood.

"Here goes nothing," Joaquin said, lifting his walkie-talkie. "Kevin, the first one's gone over. What's the status? Over."

"Nothing yet. Over."

The seconds dragged out as the wind whipped and the ceiling of fog overhead undulated and swirled. The current theory was that the cold was now keeping the fog aloft, but even if that was possible, I didn't like it. I had never thought I would wish for the eerie fog to envelop me in its chilling, hissing embrace, but having it hanging above us was almost worse. Menacing. As if it had been biding its time up there these past few days, plotting its final attack.

"The weather vane is pointing south. Over," Kevin announced.

I let out a relieved breath. At least the coins were getting this right.

"Rory, wanna go next?" Joaquin suggested.

"With pleasure."

I just wanted to get this over with so I could get back to the jail and check on Pete's status. Every second that passed that Darcy and my dad were still in the Shadowlands was a second too long. I took Ray Wagner firmly by the arm.

"Oh, so now you're getting touchy-feely with me? Is that what this is about? You got a little crush?"

I tasted bile in the back of my throat as I walked him over to the bridge. Then I grabbed his hand and turned the palm up, pressing his coin into the meaty flesh.

"This is where we say good-bye," I told him.

"Good-bye? What do you mean, good-bye?"

I turned him by the shoulders, gave him a little shove, and sent him on his way. The sucking void swallowed him whole, and we waited for the verdict.

"Pointing south again. Over," Kevin announced.

Another sigh of relief. Joaquin quickly dealt with Jack, and then Piper was the last to go. Her final words to Fisher, with a big smile, were, "Call me!"

When it was done, and the only sounds left in the world were the whistling wind and the idling noise of our car engines, we stood around, waiting. I hovered somewhere between relieved and desperately scared, because the hard part was yet to come. And from the tense looks on my friends' faces, everyone agreed on that fact.

"So when do we usher a good soul?" I said finally, voicing what everyone was thinking.

"Be advised," Chief Grantz's voice buzzed through the walkie-talkies. "The mayor is sending up one of Krista's charges with Officer Dorn. ETA two minutes."

Krista blanched. "She's what?"

"Which charge?" I asked.

"I don't know," Krista said, her voice trembling. "I didn't have anyone on the bad-guy list. What is she—"

Headlights flashed at the crest of the hill, and we turned to watch, instinctively moving into a straight line as the patrol car bumped over the potholed road. The brakes squealed as Dorn turned the car to be parallel with ours, and then he cut the engine. He stepped out, walked around the front of the car, and opened the back door. Out stepped Myra

Schwartz, the cut on her head healing nicely. She clutched her purse to her chest and looked around, not exactly scared, but intrigued.

"Where are we?"

Krista broke from the line. "Mrs. Schwartz! What're you doing here?"

"I have no idea, dear. I was hoping you could tell me," Myra said, lifting the strap of her bag onto her shoulder. Then she spotted me. "Oh, hello, Rory!"

"Hi, Myra," I replied, with a faint, strained smile.

"If you could just wait one second, I'll hopefully have an answer for you," Krista said. "Rory? Would you come with me to talk to Officer Dorn, please?" Her voice pitched up three octaves with the request.

"Sure."

We skirted around Myra and pulled Dorn toward his car. "What is going on?" Krista hissed. "She's not on the bad-guy list."

"Mayor wants to try ushering one of the good ones," Dorn said with a sniff, chewing on a piece of gum like a cow.

"What? Already?" I demanded. "Does she really think—"

"What she thinks is, we need to get things back to normal. Get this fog out of here. Clean up the beaches and figure out what the hell to do about the ferry," Dorn said tersely, looking Krista in the eye with a no-nonsense kind of glare. "If this works, it means Pete was working alone and we can be back to business as usual."

"Yeah, except my sister and my dad and at least ten other people will still be stuck in the Shadowlands," I hissed.

"Well, if things get back to normal, we can focus our energy on other things," he said pointedly. "Like getting them the hell out."

Krista hugged herself, processing this. She glanced over her shoulder at her charge, a stiff wind blowing her hair back from her face.

"So, what? Mrs. Schwartz is our guinea pig?" Krista demanded. Over by Joaquin's truck, Myra had taken out her wallet and was showing Bea and Lauren pictures of her grandkids.

"She won the lottery, yep," Dorn said, hiking up his waistband.

"But what if it doesn't work? What if she ends up in the Shadowlands?" I asked, my heart pounding.

"We'll cross that bridge when we come to it. No pun intended." Dorn smirked. Krista and I exchanged a horrified look. "Think of it this way: We're gonna have to do this sooner or later," Dorn told us. "And at least if she goes to the Shadowlands, we'll know we still have someone working against us out here."

I groaned and shook my head. "I think it's up to you, Krista. She's your charge."

Krista took a deep breath. "If the mayor thinks it's a good idea, I'm not going to contradict her." She shook her hair back and squared her shoulders. "I just hope this works."

"Good luck."

Krista smiled wanly and walked over to Myra. I saw her take the woman's hand and slip a coin into it. As I moved closer, I heard Myra thank Krista. I stood next to Joaquin, hoping for that feeling of confidence his presence usually lent me, but he took a slight sidestep away, putting a respectful distance between us. My heart ached and I stared at my toes.

"We're just going to go for a little walk, okay?" Krista said politely. "This way."

Myra smiled as Krista led her slowly toward the bridge but paused just inches from the wall of mist.

"Where am I going?" she asked Krista.

My heart nearly broke. A few weeks ago, the answer to that question would have been clear, but now . . . Krista's knees actually wavered, and for a second I thought she'd go down, but she held on somehow.

"Someplace beautiful," Krista told her with a smile. "I promise."

Myra's smile widened. Then she turned toward the mist and was gone. I instinctively reached for Joaquin's hand but caught air. He stared straight ahead, not noticing—or trying to look like he hadn't. I pinned my wrists together behind my back, straining to ignore the awful sadness welling inside my throat. In seconds, we heard the sucking sound. The mist undulated and swirled, and then everything was still.

Joaquin lifted his walkie. "Kevin? Whaddaya got? Over."

He looked me in the eye.

"Nothing yet," Kevin said. "Over."

"I can't take this," Krista whispered, her hands tepeed over her mouth. "I can't take it."

My heart seemed to pound harder with each passing second.

"Kevin?" Joaquin said.

I closed my eyes and dipped my head. My knees shook beneath me. Finally, our walkies let out a shrill peel and a crackle.

"It's pointing north," Kevin said gleefully. "The vane is pointing north!"

ALWAYS HOPE

"This is weird. I'm sorry, it's just too weird," Liam said, pacing back and forth in front of me near the foot of the bridge on Saturday morning. I rubbed my eyes and tried my best to focus. I hadn't been able to sleep in my eerily quiet house, so I'd spent half the night freezing my butt off at Pete's bedside, waiting for him to wake up. I stifled a yawn. It was Liam's first ushering, and he needed someone to guide him.

He glanced over his shoulder at his charge, Nick, who was gabbing with Fisher about his latest video-game obsession while Fisher did his best to keep up. Over at the bridge, Kevin waited while his latest charge walked through the mist.

The dawn had come today with still no sign of the sun, but the air was noticeably warmer. Instead of bundling into jeans and sweats, everyone was wearing shorts and long-sleeved T-shirts as we gathered again at the bridge, bent on getting as many people across to their final destinations as we could. Early that morning, Krista had ushered the kids over, and every last one of them had gone to the Light. Since then, the area at the base of the bridge had taken on an almost festival-like feel, with a dozen cars parked in a ragged circle, and groups of people chatting around coolers and bags of snacks. Someone's radio played fifties tunes through a car window, and a wind sock had been tied to the antenna of Bea's Jeep, its colorful stripes whipping in the breeze.

"I know. The first time is hard," I said, touching Liam's arm. He was wearing a bright red T-shirt with a white cross on the front and the word LIFEGUARD emblazoned above it. "But you're sending him to a good place. He led a good life. He's supposed to be there."

Liam nodded, but I wasn't entirely sure he was hearing me. His eyes were unfocused as he looked at the damp ground beneath our feet. I could only imagine what he was thinking. He'd been here just a few days, and he'd had so much thrown at him, most of it negative, terrifying, uncertain. Deep inside he was probably still wondering if we were crazy. If this was some kind of massive joke. My heart went out to him. It wasn't that long ago that I felt the exact same way.

"But what about Lalani? Won't she realize he's gone? Won't she be worried about him?" he asked.

I shook my head. "She won't remember him. It's part of the Juniper Landing magic. Until she gets to the Light, too, she won't even remember having had a brother."

Liam snorted a laugh. "This is insane. It's just insane."

"Liam, listen," I said, reaching for his hand. He stared down at my fingers as if he'd never seen fingers before. "What we do here, it's important. It's a calling. A mission. When we send these souls on to their final destinations, we're helping maintain the balance of the universe."

I could hear Tristan's voice in my head, telling me the same thing just a couple of weeks ago, trying to convince me.

"I know things have been out of whack since you've been here," I said, then leaned in closer. "They've actually been out of whack since I've been here, so I understand you might not exactly trust this place. But I've seen the system when it's working, and I know it's been working for a long time. It's up to us to get it back on track."

Liam sucked in a breath at the same moment the loud, sucking noise split the air and the mist around the bridge swirled. He laughed at the coincidence. Our walkies zipped to life. It was Joaquin's voice this time on the other end.

"It's pointing north. Over."

I smiled slightly. Every time I heard those words it was like a tiny piece of my shattered heart was working its way back into place. Frustratingly, Pete was still unconscious, but it was looking more and more like he'd been working alone. With him locked up safely in jail, the problem was solved. At least this particular problem, anyway. But hopefully Dorn was right. Now that we knew the ushering process was back to normal, everyone could focus on getting my dad, Darcy, and the others out of the Shadowlands.

"New guy! You're up!" Fisher shouted, clapping his massive hands together.

"You can do this," I told Liam. "You're a good person. I know you can do it."

Liam nodded. "Thanks, Rory. I'm . . . I'm gonna try."

He pushed his hands into the pocket of his plaid shorts as he walked over to join Nick. His charge turned to him with a trusting smile, his perfect white teeth practically beaming against the gray sky around us and the fog ceiling overhead. He tipped his head toward Liam as he followed him to the bridge. Whatever Liam was saying to him, it wasn't causing him any sort of alarm. And after Liam handed him the coin, Nick reached out to shake his hand.

I felt a hitch in the back of my throat as Nick crossed the threshold of the bridge and Liam waved good-bye, thinking of the night I'd said good-bye to Aaron, how happy I'd been, how Tristan and I had shared our first real kiss.

And then everything had fallen to crap.

Gravel crunched on the road, and I turned to see Tristan's SUV bouncing its way up the hill. My heart started to pound at the sight of it, and I automatically reached up to smooth my hair behind my ears. The sucking sound filled the air again, and Joaquin's voice rang out.

"It's pointing north! Yeeha!" There was a pause and then a crackle. "Sorry. Over."

Everyone laughed. Liam loped over to me just as Tristan stopped the car and slammed the door behind him. He'd showered, finally, and his blond hair hung like a shiny, healthy curtain over his blue eyes. He smiled tentatively at me as he stopped to talk to Fisher. I tore my eyes away from him long enough to hug Liam.

"Good job. See? I knew you'd be fine."

"Thanks," Liam said, blushing. "As long as he went the right way, I'm cool."

"Hey, guys."

Tristan jogged over to us, rubbing his hands together.

The sleeves of his light blue shirt were loose on his arms, and I realized he'd lost some weight during his exile. His jeans were hanging lower than usual, and there was a sharp indent to his cheeks.

"Hey," I replied, oddly shy.

"You guys, we have a problem," Lauren announced, speed-walking over to join us.

"Why am I not surprised?" I said under my breath.

"Sorry." Lauren bit her lip. "The thing is, we're running out of untainted coins. If we can't use any of the ones we got while Pete was still on the loose, we're kind of screwed."

"How many do we have left?" Tristan asked.

"I have two. Fisher has one. Kevin has one, and as far as I know, that's it," Lauren said. "Krista used most of them sending the kids across this morning."

I sighed. "Well, then we're just going to have to take it slowly. And it's going to have to stay crowded around here for a while longer."

"That sucks," Lauren said, tucking her shiny black hair behind her ears as she looked back at the bridge. "Just when things were getting back to normal."

I gritted my teeth. I was getting sick of people saying that when my sister and father and Aaron and the others were still stuck in the Shadowlands, but I didn't say anything. I knew she just wanted to feel safe again, to feel secure.

"We'll figure it out. We always do," Tristan assured her. He glanced at Liam. "Was that your first?"

"Yep. Weird," Liam said. "But Rory was a good coach."

Tristan's face lit up and my whole body responded. There was nothing like a proud smile from Tristan. "Yeah? Why am I not surprised?"

I grinned in reply.

"Told you," Tristan said. "Everything's gonna be okay."

"What the hell are you people doing up here?"

A chill raced down my spine and my eyes locked with Tristan's. I turned around slowly to find Sebastian Tse skidding down a reed-covered embankment toward us, his sister right on his heels.

"I thought the mayor dealt with these guys," Lauren said through her teeth.

"Apparently not well enough," Tristan replied, stepping in front of us.

"Where did that kid just go?" Sebastian demanded, throwing an arm out toward the bridge as he confronted Liam. "Why did you send him over that bridge by himself?"

Liam was the color of cooked lobster. "I . . . um . . . we—"

"Don't," Tristan said curtly. My heart was in my throat.

"Don't even try lying to us," Selma said, standing next to her brother, her clear blue eyes scanning our faces. "We talked to the people at our boarding house. They keep telling us about things that happened—things we should remember—like a ferry sinking? They say we were there, but neither one of us remembers it."

"How is that possible?" Sebastian said, seething, his nostrils wide as he advanced on Tristan, clearly picking him out as the leader. "What have you people done to us?"

"Why don't you let us give you a ride back to town?" Tristan suggested as Fisher and Kevin walked up behind him.

"Why don't *you* start explaining?" Sebastian shot back.

Tristan reached out a hand and gripped Sebastian's shoulder, looking him in the eye.

"Everything's fine," he said in that soothing tone I knew so well. "There's nothing sinister going on here—I promise you."

I watched Sebastian's shoulders start to relax as he looked deep into Tristan's eyes. Slowly, Tristan worked his magic on Sebastian until every ounce of his tension and doubt had been ironed away. I remembered vividly what it had felt like the first time Tristan had used his soothing power on me—how peaceful the whole world had become—and I almost felt jealous of Sebastian.

Supposedly every Lifer had this power, but Tristan was the only person I'd ever seen use it.

"You guys have had a rough few days," Tristan said. "Why don't you let Fisher drive you back? It's a long walk, especially with the mud and the downed trees."

"No way," Selma said, crossing her skinny arms over her chest. "We're not leaving here until—"

"It's just a ride, Selma," Sebastian said, lifting a shoulder. "What's the big deal?"

Her jaw dropped, but when Sebastian smiled at her, her indignation quickly faded.

"Okay," she said finally. "If you say so."

Tristan clapped Sebastian on the back as he and Fisher headed for the van, Selma trailing behind.

"Radio Joaquin," Tristan said to Kevin, sliding his hands into his pockets. "Tell him we're sending the Tses down to see the mayor again."

"On it," Kevin said, turning away.

I took a deep breath and blew it out. Crisis averted. For now, anyway.

"Um, guys? Shouldn't they not have remembered Nick?" Lauren pointed out. "The second he went over the bridge, he should have been forgotten by the visitors."

A flash of uncertainty tightened Tristan's face. "Maybe it was because they actually saw him go over? That hasn't happened before."

"Or maybe it's just one more chink in the system thanks to the unbalance of the universe," Lauren said.

"We'll figure it out," Tristan said, rubbing her back. "Hopefully it's just a blip."

"Uh, does that happen a lot?" Liam asked shakily. "People freaking out like that?"

"Not often, but when it does, we take care of it." Tristan gave a wry smile, then turned to me. "Listen, Rory, can we . . . go for a drive or something? I mean, if you don't mind me stealing her away," he said to Liam.

"No, that's cool." Liam pushed his hands into the back pockets of his shorts. "I think I'm gonna walk back to town and shake this off. Maybe find Lalani."

"You should drive down with Fisher," Tristan said. "I still don't like the idea of anyone going anywhere alone."

"Let me know if there's anything you want to talk about," I told Liam. "You know where I live, and there's always the walkies."

"Thanks, Rory," Liam said. He lifted a hand to the others in a wave and jogged to catch up with Fisher. Seconds later, Fisher's van roared out of our makeshift parking area.

"So. You ready?" Tristan asked, holding his hand out to me.

I glanced uncertainly at Lauren.

"Don't worry about me. I've got a couple more people to usher," she said, waving us off.

It felt good, just to hear someone say that. To have it not be loaded with terror and meaning. The fog was still clogging up the sky, but with each hour the air grew warmer, and I could practically feel the sun trying to make itself known again.

Things really were getting back to normal. And maybe, with Tristan's help, I'd find a way to get my family back. I took Tristan's hand and let him lead me away.

FRIEND OR FOE?

So the creepy twins are going in to see the mayor again. I wish I could be a fly on the wall for that particular conversation. I can't decide whether those two are friends or foes. They ask too many questions—that's for sure—and questions are usually a bad thing for a person in my position. But then again, if they ask too many questions of the wrong person, perhaps that person will crack and tell them the truth. That would damn them to the Shadowlands, and if I could claim them to my tally, I'd be so much closer to my goal.

I wonder if any of my so-called friends will be stupid enough to talk. There are a few who might be that dense.

Maybe I should get them drunk and see if that loosens their tongues a bit. Then I could be done with this mission by the end of the day. As long as it's not Rory. She's got another purpose to serve in this. A much bigger purpose.

THE UNIVERSE KNOWS

Tristan put the car in park and killed the engine. The windows were down, and now that we'd stopped moving, the warm, muggy air filled the space between us. He'd stopped with the nose of his SUV near the cliff where I'd once seen Joaquin, Fisher, and half a dozen other Lifers jump over the edge, to prove to me that they couldn't die. It was the same night I'd confronted Nadia for the first time. Back then I'd thought she hated me because Tristan liked me. I'd thought she was just angry, jealous, and mean.

Now I realized she'd been terrified, pulsating with fear over the world she knew and loved crumbling around her.

She was right to be afraid, and now she was gone.

"I can't get used to it," Tristan said, leaning forward to look up at the sky through the windshield. "That blanket of fog? For the first time since I arrived here, it really does feel like another world."

"That's never happened before?" I asked, fiddling with the zipper on my blue hoodie.

"No. This is new."

His hands slipped down the sides of the steering wheel and came to rest awkwardly in his lap. He caught me watching them and laughed quietly.

"You have no idea how much I want to touch you," he said.

My heart turned cartwheels. "Why don't you?"

He turned to me, his clear-blue gaze seeking something inside my eyes. "Because I don't know if you want me to."

I swallowed hard. "Tristan—"

"Hang on a sec," he said. "Just let me talk."

I nodded, unzipping my sweatshirt and tugging it free of my arms. The world suddenly felt stifling.

"When I was on the run . . . hiding out there . . . knowing everyone I'd ever cared about was hunting me down . . . I never once thought about myself," Tristan said. "I never thought about what might happen to me. What they would do to me if they found me. All I ever thought about was you."

A bubble welled up inside my throat, and I gulped it back, determined not to interrupt him.

"All that matters to me anymore is what you think of me," Tristan said. "And that you're happy. That you're okay. I spent every single night I was gone on that bridge, trying to figure out how to get the damn door or the portal or whatever it is that leads to the Shadowlands to open. Every single night. I wanted to get your dad back for you. Get Aaron back. I didn't even care if you ever found out that I was the one who saved them. I just wanted it done. For you."

I took a breath. A single tear spilled down my cheek. He reached up and touched his palm to it.

"I'm sorry that I failed you," he said.

I let out this weird noise. It was somewhere between a laugh—because how could he be apologizing to me?—and a sob—because there was so much emotion inside me that I couldn't help but release it. I reached up and held on to his forearm like I was clinging to life.

"Did you find anything?" I asked him desperately. "Anything that could help us?"

His hand dropped from my face and he held my fingers lightly between us, looking down, touching each of my fingertips in turn with the pad of his thumb. He shook his head.

"It's scary on that bridge. There are these voices—"

"You heard them, too?" I asked.

He blinked and stopped his fidgeting. "Wait. You went over the bridge?"

I nodded. "The other day. I was trying to find you. Or find a way in. I don't know. But I thought I heard . . . " I trailed off, too embarrassed to continue.

"What? Who?" he asked, breathless. "Who did you hear?"

I gulped. "My mom. And Steven Nell." I shuddered now, remembering it, and sat back in the seat, staring out over the wide blue ocean. "I thought I was going insane."

"You weren't. I mean, you're not. I heard them, too. People I knew in life, souls who came through here a hundred years ago who I'd almost forgotten. It was like they were trying to talk to me, or about me. Almost like they were laughing at me."

"Exactly." I pressed my lips together and shivered. "If it's that awful on the bridge, Tristan . . . then what's it like in the Shadowlands?"

His expression darkened, and I knew he was feeling the same pain I was. This island and the purpose he served meant more to him than anything. It must have been killing him to know that everything had gone wrong, that innocent people were suffering.

"We're going to get them back, Rory. I swear. If it's the last thing I do, I'll get them back for you."

"But how?" I asked.

"I don't know. Not yet. But I know there's an answer."

He shifted in his seat, squinting out at the blanket of fog. There was something brighter about the color of the sky. It was more purple than gray, contrasting sharply with the swirling mist overhead. I took a deep breath.

"You've always said there's no way to get into the Shadowlands. Not for us," I ventured.

"Yeah?" he said.

"But what if there was?" I asked. "If I had a tainted coin—"

"What? No. No way."

"You don't know that I can't," I shot back. "I can't know unless I try."

"Yeah, maybe. But how the hell would you get back out?" Tristan demanded.

"I'd find a way," I said, turning in my seat to face him, my pulse thrumming in my wrists. "There has to be a way."

"No way. There's no chance," Tristan said. "I am not going to let you risk your eternal soul."

"But what about—"

"No. Rory. No. I can't lose you," Tristan said, grabbing my arm. "I don't think I can exist here without you. Not anymore. You're everything to me—do you understand that? Everything."

I leaned forward, pressing my forehead to his. "Tristan—"

"Don't leave me, Rory," he whispered, his breath warm and sweet on my face. His fingers reached up and cupped my jaw, entangling themselves in my hair. "Promise me you'll never leave me."

I couldn't speak. But I looked into his eyes, so very close to mine, and I nodded. I nodded my promise until his lips met mine.

I hadn't known exactly how I would react to Tristan's kiss until this moment, but now, suddenly, I knew that I had to kiss him back with everything I had. His lips were dry and tasted of salt and something rich and warm. I felt myself start to fold into him, my whole body sighing in relief. I was home. I was home. I was home. This was where I belonged. I knew it. He knew it. I was pretty sure the entire universe knew it. So this time, I didn't pull away. I didn't think about anyone else but him. I just let him kiss me and kiss me and kiss me, until he finally came up for air.

"God, I love you," he said.

"I love you, too."

He was cupping my neck with both of his hands, and I had somehow gathered the fabric of his T-shirt up in my fists until most of his perfect six-pack was exposed. Looking into my eyes, Tristan smiled contentedly.

"Check it out."

"What?" I asked.

He turned my face to look out the windshield and I saw it. Five perfect beams of light busting through the fog ceiling, casting an incredible, ethereal glow on the ocean waves below. It was beautiful.

"The sun!" I gasped.

Tristan laughed. "The sun."

A PARTY IT IS

Tristan cranked up the stereo—some ancient tune about summer in the city—and we headed back to town with the windows down. With one hand on the wheel and the other clutching mine, Tristan looked like himself again—like the beautiful, beach-town boy I'd fallen in love with—if only slightly less tan. Suddenly the bumps and divots in the road didn't seem so much ominous as entertaining, showing us a bouncing, rollicking good time.

With Tristan's hand in mine, I knew that everything really was going to be okay. He would never give up until my father and Darcy were freed. We'd figure it out together, come up with a plan, and save them. There was no longer any doubt in my mind. When Tristan said he was going to do something, he did it.

He parked the SUV near the town square and we could already see that everyone else in Juniper Landing had been inspired with the same idea. People strolled the sidewalks, stopping to chat with one another over the abrupt change in weather, or simply tipping their faces toward the sun. A couple of guys had already whipped out a Frisbee and were busy running and leaping through the wet grass, laughing as one of them skidded on his shoulder like the world was his own personal Slip'N Slide. Liam and Lalani stood at the edge of the general store's striped awning, leaning into opposite sides of a column, not quite touching but smiling privately. There were bikers and skateboarders, joggers and gossipers. Some guy I'd never seen before bounced by on a pogo stick, giving us a jaunty wave.

The best part about it was, there were no visitors standing around shooting us dirty looks. No suspicious glances or whispers behind hands. The sun was working its magic on everyone's psyches.

"Okay, this is like a circus," Tristan said, still holding my hand.

"But in a good way," I replied. "At least there are no actual clowns."

A group of Lifers stepped out of the general store—
Fisher and Kevin included—and I smiled as they squinted
dramatically against the sun. Fisher caught sight of us, and
we walked over to meet at the center of the park. It wasn't
until we were halfway there that Joaquin shoved open the
door and slipped his sunglasses on. In the space of three
seconds, I saw him see me, saw him notice my hand clasped
with Tristan's, and watched his face go cold. I thought about
tugging my fingers out of Tristan's grip, but decided against
it. This was what I had chosen, what my heart had chosen,
and Joaquin had already given his blessing, as much as he
possibly could.

He looked both ways before crossing the street, then
jogged to catch up with us.

"How's it going, man?" Joaquin asked, slapping Tristan
on the shoulder. Tristan flinched forward from the force
of it but recovered nicely. I tried to catch Joaquin's eye, but
it was impossible with him wearing mirrored sunglasses. It
was my own distorted reflection that stared back at me.

"Okay," Tristan said. "Better now that the sun's out."

"No doubt," Fisher said, rubbing his hands together.
"You're back, the sun's back . . . . I think this calls for a cel-
ebration."

"Party on the bay beach?" Joaquin suggested, raising his
eyebrows. "Get a little beach volleyball going, maybe take

out some of the kayaks? Scrounge up some grub from the Swan and invite the visitors?"

"It's not like we can usher anyone else anyway," Kevin said, lifting his palms. "We're outta good coins."

"I see where you're going with this, but are we sure we're ready to celebrate?" Tristan asked. "Rory's family is still stuck in the Shadowlands. Not to mention a bunch of other innocent people."

Fisher seemed to deflate. The smile fell from Joaquin's lips. "What, you think I don't care about her family?" Joaquin demanded, angling himself in front of Tristan.

My heart dropped. That was a fighter's stance if I'd ever seen one. Tristan, unsurprisingly, looked confused.

"I didn't say that."

"Good, because I do care," Joaquin replied. "So what are we supposed to do? You're the one with the answers, right? Everyone's just been dying for the great Tristan to come home to give us the answers. So what do we do?"

Tristan dropped my hand. His jaw clenched and he crossed his arms over his chest. "If I knew that, don't you think I would have done it already?"

"Then why are you trying to bring us down, man? We haven't seen the sun in two weeks. I don't think hanging out and letting everyone blow off some steam for a few hours is necessarily a bad idea, considering how tense everyone's been. But if you disagree, then obviously we'll do whatever you say. Isn't that how it works around here?"

"Let's just calm down." I forced myself in between Tristan and Joaquin, my hands raised at my sides. "I, for one, think the party is a fantastic idea. We'll relax for a few hours, and who knows? Maybe Pete will finally wake up, and we can get our answers."

Joaquin simply stared at me, so I turned around to face Tristan.

"I love that you thought of my feelings, but it's okay," I told him quietly. "I think this place could use a little joy."

Tristan swallowed hard. I could feel his body unclench, letting go of the adrenaline brought out by Joaquin's obvious ire.

"Okay, then," he said to the group. "A party it is."

Half an hour later, said party was in full swing. I stood near the sidelines while Bea jumped up to spike a battered volleyball into the sand, her torso exposed in her sporty red bikini, her fiery hair loose around her shoulders. The look on her face was pure "kill." Liam and Lauren, who were playing against her and one of the taller male visitors, actually ducked for cover.

Smart move. The ball hit the ground with the force of a rocket, ricocheting off with a spray of sand and landing on the boardwalk. It almost tripped an elderly man jogging by, and he threw a curse at us as he tossed it back. Liam helped Lauren off the ground, clasping her forearm-to-forearm, and she rolled her eyes at him.

"I thought you said you were good at this," she groused.

Liam threw his sinewy arms wide. In red shorts and a white tank top, he looked every bit the lifeguard he'd been on Earth. "You could have warned me you had an Olympian on the other side."

Lauren bent to dust the sand off her legs. "She was a diver! Not a volleyball player!"

Bea and her partner cackled and shared a high five, then started whispering behind their hands, planning their next shot.

"We need more chips and salsa!" Kevin shouted. "Anybody wanna go with me?"

"I'll go!" Liam volunteered instantly, jogging off the court.

"Hey!" Lauren protested.

But Liam ignored her. He said a few words to Fisher, who stood on the opposite side. Fisher pulled his shirt off, tossed it on the sand, and went to take his place next to Lauren. Liam and Kevin took off for the stairs and disappeared up the boardwalk.

"Aw yeah! You're going down, Fish!" Bea crowed, moving her head back and forth tauntingly.

"Talk about letting off some steam," Joaquin said, moseying over and taking a long-necked bottle of beer from the cooler behind me.

I automatically glanced over my shoulder at the water. Tristan was out there, floating in a kayak alongside Teresa, their oars resting over their laps as they conversed with heads bent as close together as they could get in separate boats. I was sure Tristan was talking to her about his recovery and Pete's condition. I hoped she had only good news on both.

"Bea's pretty good, huh?" Joaquin said, gesturing at her with the bottle before popping it open on the lip of the cooler's lid.

My skin warmed at his nearness, and I sipped my water. "She's good," I agreed.

"You should see Krista play. She kicks everyone's ass." Joaquin stood next to me with forced casualness, his bare feet planted wide in the still-damp sand, one hand in the pocket of his jeans. I felt a zip of attraction and focused my gaze on the volleyball net.

"Krista? Really?"

He nodded as he took a swig of beer. "She played in high school. Coulda played in college if she'd made it that far."

Huh. Guess you could never tell everything about a person just by looking at them.

"Where is Krista, anyway?" Joaquin asked, glancing around. "She lives for this crap."

"She's cleaning up the playroom and then coming down," I told him. "Apparently the mayor's all over her to get their house back to normal now that the kids are gone."

Bea served the ball, and Fisher bumped it to Lauren, who barely got it over the net. The visitor boy on Bea's side set it up for her, and she was just going up for another spike when Fisher stood up straight, his eyes trained on the water.

"Not again."

The ball hit the sand. Everyone turned around. At the water's edge, Tristan and Teresa were just tugging their brightly hued kayaks up the sand as the fog rolled in behind them, thick and fast. I gasped, and Tristan's eyes met mine, homing in on me as if making sure he'd be able to find me once the gray mist gobbled him up.

"Who's supposed to be ushered?" Bea whispered just as we were overtaken by the billowing cloud.

I whipped around, disoriented. The fog was so thick I couldn't see more than a foot in any direction. Her voice had come from off my right shoulder when I had thought she was standing to my left.

"Bea?"

"Yeah?" she replied. I jumped. Now it sounded like she was directly behind me.

"Okay, nobody move. Just for a second." I took a breath, my pulse throbbing. I'd forgotten how terrifying the fog could be. Someone moved past nearby, the mist swirling just to my left. But there were no shadows, no shapes, no shades of light. Only fog.

I had no idea how long I stood there in silence. The fog had a way of erasing time or making it speed up or making it stop. Within it, everything was suspended. Everything except my fear.

Suddenly, someone grabbed my hand. I let out a strangled gasp.

"Tristan?" I hoped, turning around.

Joaquin appeared out of the mist, pulling my hips against his and holding me there.

"No. It's just me," he said huskily, studying my face. "I figured this might be my last chance to do this."

He leaned down and kissed me, parting my lips with his tongue, holding me against him with his strong arms. My pulse skipped erratically in exhilaration and happiness and guilt and fear. I knew in the back of my mind that I should probably break away, but my heart—my stupid, sadistic heart—demanded otherwise. I closed my eyes and gripped the back of his shirt with everything I had in me. Whether it was a good-bye or just a desperate plea for understanding, I kissed him right back.

"Ho. Lee. Crap," Fisher said.

I opened my eyes, my stomach twisting, knowing already what I would see. The fog had cleared out and Fisher was standing maybe five inches to my right, still shirtless, slowly tugging his mirrored glasses off. Joaquin released me and I stumbled backward a step, looking around. Tristan had stopped midstride, only three feet away, his face slack with devastation. I opened my mouth to say something, to explain myself, but I didn't get the chance. Our walkie-talkies crackled to life, and Dorn's voice boomed through the speakers.

"Be advised: Pete's awake."

I looked at Joaquin.

"Go," he said, the underlying meaning clear. He would handle Tristan. Whatever that meant, I'd find out later. Right now, I had a family to save.

I was halfway up the steps when Krista sprinted up to the guardrail, her blue eyes wild, half her hair falling out of her ponytail. Her face was as gray as ash.

"You guys, it's happening again," she choked out right in front of the visitors, the Lifers, everyone. "Three souls were just ushered to the Shadowlands."

ANOTHER SUSPECT

"Um . . . what's the Shadowlands?" one of the visitors asked finally.

Everyone ignored him, but the question seemed to spark something inside Tristan, who started up the beach in his bare feet, flowered swim trunks, and rash guard.

"Tristan? Where are you going?"

The look on his face as he moved past me up the steps was like nothing I'd ever seen before. At least not from him. The anger, the determination seemed to radiate from somewhere deep within him, making every step rigid, and inspiring everyone in his path to scurry out of the way.

"No, seriously. What's the Shadowlands?" the same kid repeated. I bit my lip as silence reigned. To explain it to him would mean damning him there, and damning ourselves as well. We just had to hope he'd forget about it, or else we'd take him to the mayor for a memory wipe. As long as no one answered him, we'd be okay.

I reached for Tristan's arm. He turned on me, his blue eyes bright with rage.

"You want to talk to Pete, so let's go talk to Pete," he snapped, shooting a death ray over my head in Joaquin's direction. "Let's put an end to this once and for all."

He tromped up the stairs and passed a still-stricken Krista without so much as a glance. The rest of us stood around uncertainly, a fierce breeze tearing at our clothes and whipping my hair into my eyes. Were we supposed to follow him? Did he even want us to?

I glanced at Joaquin, my heart a destroyed and pounding mess. His eyes hardened, and I felt something inside me fall away.

"So let's go," he said.

Joaquin bounded up the stairs, and the rest of us followed. Maybe Tristan had been right earlier, in the park. Maybe this party had been a bad idea. We had let our guard down. We had forgotten to be vigilant. And now we were responsible for more devastation.

"There's something else," Krista said to Joaquin as she fell into step with him. I stayed right behind them on our way up the hill, blowing by the old Victorian houses and ducking under the bowed branches of bare and spindly trees. "The twins got away from the mayor before she could wipe their memories again."

"What?" I demanded.

"So they're out there right now telling people that a bunch of locals are making people disappear at the bridge?" Joaquin said fiercely. "Great. That's the best news I've heard today."

Krista looked green. "She's got Chief Grantz looking for them, so hopefully they'll be locked up soon, too."

Joaquin upped his pace, and I trained my eyes on Tristan's back until we finally reached the town square. Tristan stormed across the park and took the steps to the police station two at a time. As he yanked open the front door, I paused to look back at the mayor's house. What had once looked like an exclusive hotel to me now seemed like the menacing witch's dark castle, another symbol of everything that was wrong with this world. The weather vane, sure enough, pointed south, obstinately ignoring the wind that swirled around it.

"What's Tristan going to do?" I asked Bea as she caught up to me. I hugged my arms against the chill.

"I don't know, but it's gonna be interesting."

We jogged across the park to catch up, blowing by Joaquin as we bounded up the marble steps. Through the lobby and down the stairs, we could hear Tristan shouting. In the time I'd known him I'd only ever heard him raise his voice once, and that was during an argument with Joaquin. Bea's eyes widened with mine as we bolted for the door at the far end. Pete was sitting facing the corner of his cell, his knees drawn up under his chin. Tristan shouted at Pete's back, crouched on the floor as close as he could get to the bars. Dorn stood in the far corner, his arms crossed over his chest as he stared everyone else down like he was Tristan's personal bodyguard.

"You killed her, Pete!" Tristan blurted, gripping the steel poles. "You killed Nadia! Do you even realize what that means? Do you know what's going to happen to you when we finally decide to usher you? Have you thought about what it's going to be like in Oblivion?"

"Tristan," Bea said softly.

The four-foot space between the outer bars of the two cells and the exterior wall of the room was now crowded with Lifers. Bea and I were closer to Tristan than anyone, having arrived first, but we were giving him a wide berth. His muscles were so taut, his teeth so tightly clenched, that I was almost afraid to touch him. He looked like a feral animal. Pete, ever so slowly, started to rock forward and back, forward and back. His forehead dipped toward his knees.

"Your only hope is to help us, Pete," Tristan continued, leaning into the bars. "That's your only hope. Because I swear to god if you don't open your mouth and start talking right now, I'll rip you out of that cell myself and send you over the bridge directly to Oblivion. I'll do it happily."

Pete let out a strangled sob. I didn't know what I had planned to say to Pete to persuade him to help us, but it wasn't this. I swallowed my fears and put my hand on Tristan's shoulder. He flinched, but then relaxed when he saw that it was me.

"Tristan, please. Listen to yourself," I whispered. He didn't move. I squatted next to him, moving my hand gently down his back. The curve of his spine, the lines of the muscles in his shoulders were visible through his shirt. "This isn't you."

His eyes darted to mine. For a second I thought he was going to contradict me, but instead, he sighed. Slowly, he stood up, tugging my hand to bring me with him.

Just then, Liam slid sideways into the room. His eyes met mine as he slunk along the back wall, trying to disappear behind the crowd of Lifers in front of him. But he wasn't fast enough to hide the fact that he was out of breath, that his white tank top was stained with sweat around the collar.

"Liam." The word was out of my mouth before I had even formed a fully coherent thought. He stopped, his red baseball cap bowed between Fisher's shoulder and Kevin's, but he said nothing.

He'd been on the beach until a few minutes before the fog rolled in, and then he'd taken off with Kevin. Kevin, who was the only one of our friends not present.

"Where were you?" I asked. "Where's Kevin?"

"I don't know," he said. "I lost him in the fog."

Pete stopped rocking at the sound of his voice. I looked back and forth between the two of them, my skin tingling with sudden suspicion. Something was going on between them. I remembered something, but whatever it was hovered on the edge of being known.

"Where did you go when you left the beach?" I asked.

Liam laughed, a sharp, bleating sound. "We went to the Thirsty Swan to look for chips and salsa, which we found, but when we came back out, I lost him in the fog. Is there a problem?"

Dorn's eyes slid back and forth from me to Liam. He sucked his teeth and narrowed his eyes.

"Then where's Kevin now?" I asked, my knees quaking. "Why isn't he here?"

"I don't know." Liam snorted. "Jeez, Rory. What's with the third degree?"

The whole time he was talking he was moving toward the door. People parted to let him through, clearly not grasping what I thought was obvious. Liam was scared. I could see it in his eyes. He was trying to act casually indignant, but he was vibrating with fear. Dorn, finally, stepped in front of him, effectively blocking his escape.

"Rory, what are you getting at?" Tristan asked. "What did he do?"

"There's something weird going on with him and Pete," I said, and then it hit me. I looked over my shoulder at Joaquin. "Yesterday, when Liam and I came here, he freaked when we thought Pete was about to wake up. And the other day, at the bridge, Pete turned around and left as soon as he saw Liam. They're hiding something."

"It's a little thin, Rory," Bea said.

"But he did jump at the chance to leave the beach when Kevin asked, and where the hell is Kevin now?" Joaquin put in.

Tristan's face turned hard. "Where's Kevin, Liam?"

"I told you, I don't know! Why don't you call him and find out?" he said, gesturing at Tristan's radio.

"I think I will." Joaquin lifted the walkie-talkie to his lips and pressed it to speak. "Kevin? You there, buddy? Over."

He released the button. Nothing but a low, distant hum of static. Everyone eyed Liam, who was rapidly turning white.

"Anyone seen Kevin? Over," Joaquin asked.

Silence.

"Dorn," Tristan said. "Lock him up."

Liam made a move like he was going to bolt, but there was no getting around Dorn, whose massive hands came down on his shoulders and dragged him backward.

"No. You can't do this!" Liam shouted. "I have rights." He looked around desperately. "Don't I? Don't I have rights?"

With one swift motion, Fisher had the door of the second cell open. He held it while Dorn tossed Liam inside and then closed it with a clang. Liam practically threw himself at the bars. Bea glanced around at the crowd. Everyone was looking disturbed or unsure or murderous or a combination of the three.

"Maybe I should clear the room?" she suggested.

"Good idea," Tristan said.

Bea managed to gather everyone back through the door and into the hallway, herding them up like cattle. When the door closed behind her, only Tristan, Dorn, Krista, Joaquin, and I were left. Liam's pleas fell silent. He sat down on the cot. The bed squeaked beneath his weight, and he leaned his head against the bars, scowling across the way at Pete.

"I can't believe this is happening," he said.

Pete was as still as stone.

"Just tell us where you went after you left the Thirsty Swan," I said, lifting my shoulders. "How hard is that?"

"I went to find Lalani," he snapped, his eyes flashing. "Satisfied now? Can I go?"

"How?" Joaquin asked.

"How?" Liam repeated.

"Yes, how?" Krista asked, tucking her hair behind her ears. "No one can see half a foot through the fog. How were you going to find her?"

"Carefully?" Liam shot back in an uncharacteristically sarcastic tone.

"Did you find her?" I asked.

"Yes," he snapped. "And you were wrong, by the way. She does remember her brother, and she's wondering where the hell he is."

Tristan and I locked eyes. So the Tses weren't just a blip.

Liam shot me a disgusted look and turned away. "I'm not saying anything more to you."

"Liam—" I started.

"No!" he snapped, shoving himself to his feet. "I trusted you. You made me trust you! And you lied to me! And now you throw me in here? Who the hell do you think you are?"

His hand shot through the bars and I jumped back. Joaquin grabbed his wrist and twisted until Liam's knees hit the floor, his face contorted in pain. I pressed myself back against the wall, gasping for air as Joaquin leaned in toward the top of Liam's bowed head.

"You even try to touch her again and you'll be sorry."

Krista and I looked at each other, stunned.

"Dude," Tristan said. "Release."

Joaquin gritted his teeth but let go of Liam's arm. As he stood up, Liam drew his hand into his chest and held it there, curling in on himself like a startled snail pulling back into its shell.

"Maybe . . . maybe we should go get some air," Tristan suggested, looking around at the rest of us. "Go outside and talk this through?"

"Strategize," Dorn said, his eyes like slits. "I like it."

"We can't just leave the two of them in here together," Joaquin pointed out.

"I'll stay," Krista offered, holding her chin up bravely. Even pale and sweaty, she still managed to look like a supermodel.

Dorn clapped her on the side of her arm, and she staggered sideways into the bars of Pete's cell. "If you need us, you've got your walkie."

Krista nodded, tugging it out of her dress pocket and cocking it at him like a gun. "I got it."

As I followed the guys out of the room, I looked back over my shoulder at Liam one last time as he gripped the bars and glared at Pete, the fury plain on his face.

HANDS ON

Outside the wind was whipping furiously. A pair of women walking out of the beauty-supply store screamed as a scrap of wood shingle came flying at them. They clung to each other and ducked, just narrowly avoiding some serious head injuries as the scrap slammed into the front window. A few visitors sat inside the picture window at the general store, staring out at the horizon, the pads of one man's fingers pressed into white dots against the glass. When I turned to look, I saw slate-gray storm clouds gathering over the bay.

We hadn't gotten one full day of sun. Not even a day.

"This is not good," Tristan said, pausing next to the swan

fountain at the center of the park. Even its shallow water was rippling in the wind. Bea, Fisher, Lauren, and a crowd of other Lifers huddled under the awning of the bike shop, watching us, waiting for direction. "It's starting to feel like the Jessica time around here."

"Dude, please. This is nothing like that," Joaquin shot back.

"Are you kidding me?" Tristan demanded, his long blond bangs blown back from his face. "You just nearly broke some kid's arm when we have zero proof that he did anything wrong."

"Oh, so you would have rather let him get his hands on Rory?" Joaquin replied.

"Well, if you want me to kick the ass of every guy who puts his hands on Rory . . . " Tristan said, getting right up in Joaquin's face.

"Step back, Tristan," Joaquin said, pushing Tristan backward.

"No. I don't think I will." Tristan shoved Joaquin with both hands.

"You guys. Don't!"

But it was too late. Joaquin pulled back and threw a punch at Tristan's face. I screamed as it landed with a crack across Tristan's jaw, sending him reeling sideways into Dorn's chest. Dorn caught him, and I expected him to hold Tristan back or get between the two of them, or at least hold Tristan back, but he merely turned Tristan around and gave him a little push, sending him back for more.

"Dorn!" I shouted.

He gave a little shrug as Tristan threw himself at Joaquin's midsection. Joaquin was flipped off his feet and hit the walkway on his back. For a second he lay still, his eyes wide open, gasping for air. Tristan had knocked the wind right out of him.

"Tristan! Stop!" I shouted as Tristan straddled Joaquin and cocked his right fist. He froze, and I wrapped my arms around his shoulders, pulling him away from Joaquin. "Get off him! He can't breathe!"

The wind flung my hair across my eyes and into my mouth as I dragged Tristan away. Dorn knelt down and helped Joaquin sit up, and he finally sputtered and coughed, dragging in a long, ragged breath with his hand to his chest. The clouds had moved in fast, blocking out the sun and casting everything in their dull gray shadow. A circle of crows cawed merrily overhead as if beckoning the storm our way.

Joaquin took a few deep breaths, looking up at me as he struggled to get control. He grasped Dorn's arm and staggered to his feet. "I'm going to see if I can track down Kevin," he said, then turned to Dorn. "You, don't let the new kid out of his cell."

Dorn nodded curtly. "Got it."

"Why don't you guys go get some rest?" Joaquin added, looking at Tristan and me. "We can meet at the mayor's in the morning and discuss our options."

"Options?" Tristan said, his chest still heaving.

Joaquin laughed, shaking his head. "You know what I'm talking about, Tristan. You saw the way Pete was acting in there. He's not gonna say anything, and this place is going to hell in a handbasket. We have to discuss our options."

Tristan's jaw set, his eyes grim. "We can't—"

"Dude, the guy hit you over the head with a baseball bat. He almost killed you. He *did* kill Nadia and possibly Cori, too. He betrayed us. Everything you believe in. And the only way to fix it is to get him to talk." Joaquin paused. He took a step toward Tristan, whose hands automatically coiled into fists. Joaquin held up his palms.

"Just think about it," he said. "That's all I'm asking. Take the night to think about it." Then he looked up at the blackening sky. "If we even have that long."

He turned around and stormed off toward the others on the far sidewalk to give out orders. Tristan took a few cleansing breaths, then glanced at Dorn.

"If he finds Kevin, let me know," he said.

"Will do," Dorn replied. "But I'm sure he'll contact you on the walkie."

Tristan looked off after Joaquin. "Yeah, I'm not so sure about that."

He took one step in the direction of his house, but I stopped him, clasping his wrist with both hands. He looked down at my fingers, then ever so slowly, trailed his gaze along my arm, up to my shoulders, and finally met my eyes.

"You're not going home," I said, tense with the fear of rejection, no matter how determined my words were.

"No?" he asked. "Where am I going?"

I released his wrist and trailed one hand down to entwine my fingers with his. "You're coming with me."

TWO HEARTS

By the time we got back to my house, the wind was so intense we had to cling to each other as we turned down Magnolia and staggered toward the gate. Dead leaves and flower petals scraped our faces, and a scrap of paper slapped against my leg, wrapping itself around my calf and staying there as I reached for the latch. The second I released it, the gate flew open, slamming back into the fence and cracking off its hinges. Tristan grabbed for it, but there was nothing he could do. It tumbled end-over-end down the street and crashed into the side of a neighboring house.

"Let's get inside," he said.

I nodded, and together we hunched forward, sprinting up the front walk. My hands shook as I unlocked the door, and Tristan clung to it so it wouldn't meet the same fate as the gate. He pulled it closed behind us and turned the lock. Inside, I flicked on the first three lights I came to. Tristan followed and we met in the center of the living room, facing each other over the two-foot breadth of the wooden coffee table.

I felt queasy and nervous. An hour ago, Tristan had caught me kissing another guy—his best friend. And now here we were, alone. No matter what I said, it would never be enough. But I had to try.

"Tristan," I began. "About Joaquin."

He closed his eyes, as if the very sound of the name caused him pain, and held up one hand. "Don't."

"No, I want to explain," I insisted.

A gust of wind hit the house so hard it moaned, then let out a series of loud snaps and crackles as ancient beams and floorboards resettled. I took a step around the side of the table and felt buoyed when Tristan didn't move.

"I'm not going to stand here and say I don't care about him, because I do." I swallowed hard, gripping my fingers in front of me. "I wouldn't have made it through the last week without him."

Tristan stared at me, his face a complete blank.

"But the second I saw you again, the second I touched you, I knew . . . it's you. It's always been you. With Joaquin, it—"

"Stop," Tristan said.

I froze in my tracks. I'd been inching toward him the whole time I was talking, and now I hovered just inches away, so close I could see the glint of the blond stubble beneath his jaw. My gaze flicked to his hands.

Reach for me, I willed him. *Please. Just—*

"So you don't want him. You don't want to be with him?"

"No," I said, closing the distance between us. "I want you."

His jaw worked and his fingers clenched. I could see, could *feel* how hard it was for him to hold back. "Are you sure? You'd better be sure about this, Rory, because we're going to be here forever, the three of us. If you change your mind . . . it would torture you—torture all of us— forever."

I gazed into his blue eyes, my heart thrumming inside my chest. Slowly, carefully, gently, I reached out to touch my fingertips to his chest. "I want this. I want you. Forever."

Tristan let out a shaky, relieved sigh. He ran both his hands over my head and down the long, tangled braid of my hair. "I am in love with you, Rory Miller," he said, using my real name, which sent a thrill right through me. "All I want is to be with you."

I smiled and realized that I was crying. "All I want is to be with you," I replied.

"Just try to get rid of me," Tristan said with a grin.

Then he leaned down to touch his lips to mine, and I felt the urgency of his kiss run through me, filling every inch of me, warming my body from head to toe with an insistent, throbbing heat. I pressed up against him, pouring every ounce of the fear and frustration, of the misunderstanding and longing I'd felt over the past two weeks into my kiss. I had missed him so much. I had wanted to believe in him so much. And now he was here and he was true and he was mine.

For that one infinitesimal second I didn't care about Pete or Liam or the universe or the Shadowlands or anything other than this. Then our walkie-talkies suddenly let out a freakish peal, and Krista's panicked voice filled our little cocoon.

"Mayday! Mayday! Emergency! Or whatever! Over!"

We both whirled around as erratic pounding sounded on the front door. Tristan darted for it. I fumbled for my radio, which was clipped to the side of my waistband, and pressed down on the red button.

"What is it, Krista? Over."

"It's the visitors! Over!"

The front door opened, and Krista stumbled inside, soaked to the bone.

"The visitors what?" I said, dropping the walkie-talkie on the floor. "What about them?"

Krista gulped, bracing one hand on the entryway table. "We have a situation," she said. "The visitors have taken over the town square."

MALLEABLE

Even knowing how overcrowded the island had become, nothing could have prepared me for the horde that greeted us when we reached the town square. The visitors covered every inch of the park, some standing on benches, others clumped around lampposts. People streamed out of the general store to join the throng, standing on their toes and craning their necks even in the driving rain, trying to see what was going on.

Up front, of course, were the Tses, standing near the stone rim around the swan fountain, holding court with a willing group of visitors. From this distance, I couldn't hear them, but Sebastian gestured angrily with his hands, and a few members of his audience nodded, agreeing with whatever he was saying.

"Damn. This doesn't look good." Tristan stopped at the corner of Freesia Lane and the square, his face going pale.

Joaquin, Fisher, and Kevin skirted around the edge of the crowd, catching angry looks from a group of young men in ponchos as they jogged over to join us. Ursula and Chief Grantz slipped away from the grocery stand to gather behind us as well.

"Kevin!" Krista exclaimed. "You're alive!"

"Yeah, I'm fine. When the fog came in and I lost Liam, I figured I'd head home to wait it out," he said. "I must have fallen asleep. Sorry. Joaquin told me you guys were worried about me."

"We're just glad you're okay," Tristan said, clapping him on the shoulder.

A few other Lifers circumvented the park, sticking to the outer sidewalks, and joined us, everyone drawn to Tristan like moths to a flame. Lauren and Bea jogged over from the direction of the docks.

"Speaking of Liam," Fisher said, "we have a problem." He took a breath and held it for a second before delivering the news. "He's gone."

"Gone?" I exclaimed. "How?"

"Officer Dorn had my key. He left his post for five seconds when some visitors came into the station, demanding to make long-distance calls," Grantz said. "When he got back down there, Liam was gone, and it was only then that he noticed the key was gone, too. Someone let him out. But of course Pete's not talking, so . . . "

Tristan paced away from us, his fists shaking at his sides. His hair was slicked down across his forehead, and the rash guard he'd had on ever since we'd left the beach clung to his chest in the rain.

"Who the hell is doing this?" he demanded.

"I'd say at this point, that's only one of our problems," Fisher said, eyeing the crowd.

"Why don't we just start ushering them?" Ursula suggested, lifting a tissue to her nose to cover a sneeze. "Some of them are ready to cross, and if we could thin out the crowd . . . "

"We can't," Joaquin told her. "We ran out of coins earlier. No one's leaving here anytime soon."

"Okay," Tristan said, gathering himself. "First things first. We have to find Liam. Bea, Rory, you get twenty or so people together and fan out to search the island. He doesn't know it as well as we do, so it shouldn't take long to find him. Fisher and Kevin, get a dozen of our biggest guys and get up to the bridge. Whatever happens today, he's not bringing any more innocent souls to the Shadowlands."

"Don't you want me here for crowd control?" Fisher asked, shoving his fist into his open palm.

"Dorn, Grantz, Joaquin, and I will handle it," Tristan said. He looked over at the burgeoning mob, who let out a cheer at something Sebastian had just said. "I'm going to go talk to them."

"What are you going to say?" Joaquin asked.

"I'll figure it out. And if it doesn't work, we could always try using the soothing power on them. Between the four of us, we should be able to subdue the worst of them. We'll just infiltrate the park and start working the crowd." Tristan glanced at Fisher and Bea. "We're wasting time. Go!"

"We're on it, T," Fisher said. He lifted his dark hood over his head and led the others over to a line of waiting trucks and cars parked down one of the side streets, their headlights shining through the rain as their windshield wipers flapped frantically.

"This is my fault," Krista said, shifting from foot to foot under the waterlogged awning. "I should have stayed at the station to relieve Dorn if he needed me. I was just so tired, and he told me to go home. . . . "

"Krista, it's okay." Tristan gripped her shoulder, and she stopped wavering. "Don't worry. We'll find him."

He looked up at me, a raindrop working its way down his cheek like a tear. "You didn't want to go with Bea?"

"I'd rather stay close to you," I said, glancing around warily as a pair of visitors slowly walked by, staring us down.

Tristan reached out and squeezed my hand. "Wish me luck."

"Good luck," Krista and I chorused.

He gave a nod to the men, and Grantz and Joaquin fell into step behind him as he crossed the street toward the park. Joaquin lifted his radio and told Dorn to join them. Krista grabbed my hand to tug me toward the police station. Its marble columns faced the back of the swan fountain, and as we climbed the steps I realized the brilliance of her plan. From here we would be dry under the station's stone overhang and still see everything, including Tristan as he stepped up next to Sebastian.

"Rory?" Krista said, shivering next to me as Tristan put his hand on Sebastian's back. "I'm scared."

I nodded, my teeth chattering. "Me too."

She squeezed my hand as Tristan hopped up onto the fountain's edge so that he was a couple of heads above the crowd. He lifted both of his hands, trying to quiet the din. Suddenly the doors behind us burst open, and Dorn barreled out, rushing down the stairs to join Grantz and Joaquin at the fountain.

"Please, everyone!" Tristan called out. "Please, calm down."

"Who the hell are you?" the large bearded man from the twins' boarding house shouted.

"My name is Tristan Parrish," he replied. "I'm the mayor's son. And I'd be glad to answer your questions and hear your concerns."

The crowd roared, everyone trying to speak at once. Sebastian and Selma exchanged a glance behind Tristan's back.

"Now, you know I can't understand any of you if everyone talks at the same time," Tristan said with a casual, indulgent smile. "If you wouldn't mind raising your hands, I can repeat your question for everyone to hear and then do my best to answer it."

Three dozen hands shot into the air.

"He's good," I said under my breath.

"Yeah, but how good?" Krista asked, her knees knocking together beneath her white raincoat. She glanced back over her shoulder at the double doors to the station. "Um . . . Rory? Is anyone with Pete right now?"

My heart dropped into my toes. Someone had Grantz's key. Whoever it was could be doubling back there right now to let Pete out, too.

"Let's go."

Krista grabbed my hand as we tore inside the police station, our sneakers squealing and squishing the whole way across the marble lobby. Together we ran down the hallway, and I yanked open the door. My lungs released a relieved sigh when I saw that Pete was still there, still sitting on the floor with his arms around his legs. A streak of dirt cut across one cheek, and his eyes looked bloodshot. He glanced up at us as we walked in, following Krista with his eyes as she slipped by me to perch on a stool in the far corner.

"Good. You're still here," I said.

"Where would I go?"

I froze at the sound of his voice, low and crackly and dry. This was the first time anyone had heard him speak since Thursday night. My pulse throbbed inside every inch of my skin. This was my chance. The chance I'd been waiting for. I dropped to my knees and gripped the bars in front of me. They were so cold my fingers ached.

"Pete, how did Liam get out?" I demanded. "Did someone help him? Did he tell you where he was going?"

Pete ever so slowly peeled his eyes off Krista and slid his gaze to my feet.

"No."

"Pete, come on. Enough is enough," I said. "Don't you want to talk? Don't you want to tell someone what's going on? Don't you want to get the hell out of here?"

He bit his lip and stared. There was something so vulner-able about him, so malleable, and I realized suddenly—that was exactly what Pete was. He'd been the last young Lifer to arrive here before Krista, who was the last to arrive before me, Darcy, and Liam. He was still just a kid like me. Someone who had been promised something he sorely wanted. Suddenly, my heart went out to him. Even with everything he had done, he was still one of us. He was still human.

"Darcy was always nice to you, wasn't she, Pete?" I said quietly. "She laughed at your jokes, she thought you were fun, and she loved your music."

Pete's eyes flicked up to meet mine, and I could see some-thing shifting within them. He was starting to cave. I clung to the bars and held my breath.

"She doesn't deserve what she's suffering right now, Pete. You know it. I know it. But only you know how to get her back. Please, just tell me how to save my sister."

Pete pressed his lips together. His grip on his arms tight-ened. Outside, muted by the thick walls, a communal jeer went up from the crowd. I darted a glance at Krista, who looked as worried as I was. Time was slipping away from us, faster and faster and faster. If we didn't fix this soon, those people out there were going to make what happened with Jessica look like a cakewalk.

"You just got in over your head a little bit," I said to Pete, trying to keep the desperation out of my voice. "You believed a promise someone made to you, and it forced you to do bad things. But if you help me, you're going to redeem yourself in everyone's eyes." I took a shaky breath. "If you help me, I'll help you. I'll speak for you with the others."

Pete swallowed. He rested his chin atop his arm and stared straight ahead. Not at me, not at Krista. At nothing.

"Eighteen paces," he said quietly.

Krista stood up, the stool screeching against the floor and knocking back against the wall. "What?"

Pete was still as stone. "You have to walk exactly eighteen paces onto the bridge," he said. "Then turn to the left and whisper the worst sin you committed in life. That's how you open the door to the Shadowlands."

I stood up, every cell in my body on fire. "That's it?"

"As long as you tell the truth, the door will open," Pete said, hazarding a glance at my face. He sniffled and rubbed his nose.

The surprise inside me manifested itself into one big, choking laugh.

"And then? How do we get the innocents out?" I asked.

"If a Lifer opens the door on purpose, for pure intentions or whatever, anyone who doesn't belong in the Shadowlands will be set free."

"Are you sure that's all we have to do?" I asked, my skin on fire with anticipation. "There's no price?"

"Nope. I guess the powers that be or whatever figured no Lifer would ever be crazy enough to try it."

"Well, this one is." I dropped to my knees again to be at eye level with him. "Thank you, Pete. Honestly. You have no idea what this means to me." I reached out and clasped his forearm. "Thank you."

Then I jumped up and grabbed the door handle. "Let's go!"

"What? No way," Krista replied. "You're totally out of your mind. Who says he's telling the truth? Who says you're not gonna just get sucked into the Shadowlands, too?"

"Krista—"

"No. There's no way I'm letting you do this without backup," she said, shaking her head as she tugged out her walkie-talkie. She hit the button to speak, but I closed the gap between us with one long stride and grabbed her arm.

"Don't."

"Rory."

"Krista, they're going to try to stop me, and I won't let them." I snatched the walkie-talkie out of her hand and turned it off. "I'm going to the bridge, and I'm going to get my family back."

I stared her straight in the eye. "Now, are you coming with me or not?"

DARK AS PITCH

"Please don't do this, Rory. Please. You're my best friend on this stupid island. I don't want you to get stuck in the Shadowlands."

"I won't, Krista," I told her, even though, technically, I had no idea what was about to happen.

Her cold fingers closed around my wrist as we slipped out the back door of the police station. The mayor's car was parked just a few yards away. "How do you know that?"

My stomach clenched and I braced myself, trying not to look as terrified as I felt. "I just do," I lied.

Another loud roar of anger went up from the crowd out

front. Krista and I both froze, and my knees went weak. Tristan had lost them somehow. My eyes darted toward the front of the building, and I hesitated.

"Tristan?" Krista breathed.

I clenched my jaw. This was not the time to go running to my boyfriend's side. I finally had the information I needed to save my father and Darcy. We each had a role to play, and mine was not here in town. It was up at the bridge. If I could just get there, if I could just free my family and the other innocent souls, everything would go back to normal. We could usher the visitors and set things right.

"We can't help him," I said. Someone shrieked angrily and a cheer rose up. "If anything goes wrong, they'll get him somewhere safe. Don't worry. Now, give me the keys."

Krista's eyes were wide and teary. "Please, Rory. Don't make me. If something happens to you—"

"Give me the keys!" I snapped, frustrated.

Krista flinched, and a single, fat tear rolled down her face. She sniffled and drew the keys out of her pocket. Guilt consumed me, but I still snatched them away from her.

"I'm sorry, but I have to go," I said, heading for the car. "The sooner I get up there, the sooner this is over."

Krista hesitated, looking back and forth between me and the front of the building, as if she could see what was going on with Tristan. I had a feeling that, in the back of her mind, she was wondering whether she could get through the town square and up to her house alive so that she could hide under the covers until someone came to tell her everything was okay. Then another roar of ire rose up, and she bolted toward the car. When she climbed in beside me, she was soaking wet and crying.

I bit down on my tongue, gunned the engine, and headed for the hills.

"No way, Rory. Not gonna happen."

Fisher proved to be a tough sell on the whole *opening the door to the Shadowlands* question. He stood between me and the bridge like my personal Great Wall of China, his legs planted firmly apart, his massive arms crossed over his chest as rain poured freely over his closely-shaved head and down his face and into the collar of his T-shirt. The guy had lost the jacket at some point, and now stood there with nothing but the gray tee sucked to his every muscle, and cargo pants that were soaked through to a dark shade of green. In another life, this guy could have made a killing as a professional wrestler. He just needed to get himself a few well-placed tattoos and a stupid nickname, and he was gold.

"Fisher, don't you want me to get Darcy back?" I asked, trying to bite back the frustration simmering inside me.

"She's being tortured right now. While you're just standing there."

Kevin and the other guys were lined up next to Fisher like a barricade, but none of them were quite as intimidating. Without Tristan or Joaquin here, Fisher was the de facto leader, and I knew that if I could get through to him, the others wouldn't fight me. I glanced sidelong at Krista. Her white rain jacket was snapped up to her chin, the hood forming a perfect O around her face with the laces pulled taut. She looked like she would rather be anywhere other than here.

"Look, my orders were not to let anyone over the bridge, so I'm not letting anyone over the bridge," Fisher told me.

"Well, there you go!" Krista said, reaching for my hand. "Let's go back to my house."

I snatched my fingers away. An impressive fork of lightning split the sky behind Fisher, and a crack of thunder quickly followed, causing Krista to yelp.

"But I'm not just anyone," I replied, clenching my fists, the skin on my hands so raw it tightened to near cracking. "I'm the person Pete finally talked to."

Fisher narrowed his eyes and reset his stance, looking down his nose at me like he was the commanding officer and I was some pissant private challenging his authority.

"Right. And how am I supposed to know that for sure,

exactly?" he asked. "How do I know you're not just making this up?"

Now I glared at Krista. It was way past time for her to speak up. But she just looked at me, her blue eyes wide like a startled rabbit's.

"Tell him, Krista!" I demanded. "Tell him what you heard."

Krista looked at the ground. "He said that if we opened the door, the innocents would be released," she mumbled. "But I don't get why it has to be you, Rory!" she whined, suddenly full of life. "Can't we send one of the older Lifers over? Someone who doesn't have friends or a family or—"

"We don't have time to start looking for a willing guinea pig!" I interjected. "Don't you get it? It's my family in there. My best friend. We have to do this now."

A few of the other guys heard this and started to whisper, looking at us with a new sort of respect. Possibly awe.

Suddenly, Krista's face hardened into a sort of resolute mask of fear. "Fine. Then I'm coming with you."

"What?" Fisher, Kevin, and I said as one.

Krista cleared her throat and spoke up. "There's no way I'm going to stay back here and explain to Tristan how I let her go alone," she said. "Dealing with the fallout from that would be way worse than anything the Shadowlands has to offer."

"Wow, Krista. I'm impressed," Fisher said, looking her up and down.

Krista lifted her shoulders. "She's my best friend. Like my sister. If she goes, I guess I have to go."

Kevin turned his back to us and murmured something in Fisher's ear. Then Fisher turned his back on us, and the two of them got into it, whisper-fighting something fierce until Fisher finally shouted, "Fine!"

I felt Krista tense up. "Fine what?" I asked.

"Fine, you guys can go. But I'm coming with you. Safety in numbers, right?"

He stepped aside, forming a hole in the line between him and Kevin. The bridge loomed before us, the steel girders seeming huge at the foot of the bridge before they tapered up and disappeared inside the swirling gray mist. My throat went dry, and the mixture of fear and adrenaline coursing through me made my head swim. But I forced myself to walk toward the seam where the muddy road met the steel ramp, and I didn't look back, though I could hear Krista and Fisher behind me.

I stopped in front of the wall of mist. Eighteen paces and I'd see Darcy again. Eighteen paces and I'd have my dad back. And Aaron and Jennifer and everyone else who was needlessly suffering. Fisher stepped up to my left, Krista to my right.

"I should warn you guys, it's not pleasant in there," I said. "There are voices. Whispers. And something kept trying to grab me. I don't know who or what, but . . . it wasn't fun."

"I think I'm gonna be sick," Krista said.

"Don't worry," Fisher told her, giving her shoulder a squeeze. "I got your back."

I took a deep breath. "Ready?"

Fisher looked over his shoulder and gave Kevin a nod. Kevin lifted his walkie to his lips and spoke. "Joaquin. Come in, Joaquin. Rory, Krista, and Fish are going over the bridge. They say they know how to open the portal to the Shadowlands. You might want to get your ass up here."

"Fisher!" Krista and I scolded.

Fisher shrugged. "You don't go into battle without backup. Now, let's go rescue my girlfriend."

And then he took the first step into the mist. I clenched my teeth and followed him, knowing that Joaquin and possibly Tristan—if he could get away—were already on their way here, but it didn't matter anymore. This wasn't going to take long. By the time he got here, it would all be over.

The second the fog enveloped me, I was alone. Fisher should have been dead ahead, Krista to my right, but I couldn't see either one of them. Then, suddenly, a hand closed around mine and Krista reappeared. She smiled wanly and I smiled back.

"Here goes."

Together, we began to count our steps.

"One . . . two . . . three . . . "

The whispers began.

" . . . *she's brought a friend* . . . "

" . . . *pretty, pretty* . . . "

" . . . *bite the toes off one by one* . . . "

Krista's grip on my hand tightened. Fear coursed through me, pulsating through my veins, my temples, my wrists, my heart, but I knew I couldn't stop. Darcy was depending on me. My dad and Aaron needed me. I imagined their faces, their smiles, their eyes, and kept walking. I'd survived this once before. I could survive it again. For them.

"Four . . . five . . . "

A cold finger swept along my cheek. Krista yelped and swatted at the back of her neck.

"What was that?" she whined.

"It's nothing. It's just messing with us," I told her, willing the terror out of my voice.

"*What's* messing with us?" Her grip on my hand was like a vice.

"The bridge," I said through my teeth. "Just keep going. We're almost there."

"Six . . . seven . . . eight . . . " I counted on my own this time.

"...*still so clueless*..."

"...*doesn't know what she's*..."

"...*dark as pitch, that one*..."

"Rory?" Krista mewled, looking over her shoulder at nothing. "This was a bad idea. I wanna go. Let's go, okay? Please?"

Then she screeched again, and I saw her hair rise up behind her, some invisible thing in the mist pulling at its matted strands.

"Oh my god," she whined, her breath broken. "Oh my god, oh my god, oh my—"

"There's nothing there," I promised her. "Keep moving."

"Nine . . . ten . . ."

The mist to my left swirled, then started to pulse. In and out. In and out. As if someone was standing just inches away, breathing. Watching. Krista held my hand with both of hers now, pulling me awkwardly against her side.

"Fisher?" I whispered.

The response was a laugh so dark and evil it couldn't have belonged to a human being. At least not a living one. My brain went momentarily fuzzy, and I was sure I was about to pass out from the fear. But Krista clung to my side, steadying me with her terror and forcing me to be the brave one. I knew I couldn't go down. If I went down, all was lost.

"You don't need them. Your family. You don't," Krista

whispered furtively, staring at the pulsating mist. "You've
got me now. And Tristan, Joaquin. Darcy and your dad were
going to move on anyway, right? Why don't you just let it
go? Just let it go so we can get the hell out of here?"

I clenched my teeth and ignored her. I had to. If I listened
to what she was saying I was going to punch her in the face.
I turned and kept walking, now dragging Krista with me.

"Thirteen . . . fourteen . . . fifteen . . . sixteen."

"Nononononono," Krista babbled, shaking her head.
"No, please. No."

"*. . . come out, come out, wherever you are!*"

"*. . . never ever thought it would end this way . . .*"

"*. . . closer, dearie, just a little closer . . .*"

A bony finger swiped my ear from top to bottom, tucking stray hairs behind it. I felt a chill down my back and
almost squealed. Krista planted her feet and leaned backward, doing her best to root me to the spot. Luckily, I was
stronger. I closed my eyes and took the last two steps, yanking on her arm.

"Seventeen," I said. "Eighteen."

We stopped. Krista shook from head to foot. I could hear
her teeth chattering. I gathered every bit of courage I had
left within me, my heart pounding so hard I could feel little
else, and turned to the left. There was no sign of Fisher.
Whatever he thought he might save us from, it wasn't going

to happen. We were on our own. Hopefully he'd just keep walking and find himself right back where he'd started, as I had two days ago.

"Roreeeee . . . " Krista called out. Sweat had pooled between our palms and turned to ice.

"Don't worry. Everything is gonna be fine."

This was for my family. This was for my dad and Darcy and Aaron. As much as I hated to think of him at that moment, I closed my eyes and conjured up a picture of Steven Nell, gasping and sputtering as he took his very last breaths. I held my own breath and whispered, "I took another person's life."

There was a loud bang, like the sound of a dump truck lowering its metal lift to the ground without care. The bridge beneath us shook. Krista somehow tightened her grip on me, squeezing my fingers until I thought my hand would shatter. The mist in front of us started to move, haphazardly at first, like smoke being waved off a fire, but it quickly organized itself into a vortex, swirling before us like a sideways tornado opening its mouth. We stood there, but we felt no wind.

I was staring at an endless depth of blackness, darker than anything I'd seen on Earth, and I was sure that I had been duped. I was certain that at any second, something cold and gray and slimy was going to reach out and grab me and Krista and drag us into hell.

She was going to spend eternity suffering in the Shadowlands, and it was my fault.

"Krista," I said through my teeth. "Run."

"What?" she whined.

I was about to turn and push her as hard as I could back into the mist, but then—right then—I heard her. Her voice was so close she couldn't have been more than two feet away.

"Rory! You came!"

"Darcy!"

I reached into the darkness—reached toward the voice—and my fingers found cloth. A sleeve. I dug my fingernails into it as hard as I could and pulled. I had her. I had Darcy. Then the person I was clinging to appeared, and it wasn't Darcy.

It was Steven Nell.

He looked exactly the same as he had the last time I'd seen him. The stringy dark hair falling over his forehead. The thick glasses perched on his nose. The cruel smile on his thin, pale lips.

Suddenly time stopped. I felt the blade of his knife in my stomach as if it had just happened. Saw the blood in my sister's hair. My father's body crumbling to the ground. It was as if every nightmare I'd had for the past month was suddenly coming to life in vivid, horrifying, excruciating detail.

"Rory Miller," he said gleefully. "You've come home."

Suddenly I knew. He wanted to do it again. He was going to do it again. He was going to murder us, slaughter us, over and over and over again for as long as the universe existed. Until the end of time. He was looking forward to it.

I let go of him and ran. Right into Krista.

She looked up at me, her blue eyes dark with rage.

"Krista?" I whispered.

"Welcome to the Shadowlands, Rory."

Then she shoved me with a strength I never would have imagined she had in her, right into Steven Nell's waiting arms.

WILLINGLY

I stared at Krista, feeling Steven Nell's awful breath warming the back of my neck. She was the accomplice? It wasn't possible. She was my friend. My best friend. I'd treated her like a sister, and she had done the same for me. How could she have done this? How could she have tried to pin everything on me, dragged my family to the Shadowlands, plotted behind our backs, and lied to our faces?

Krista smoothed her wet hair back from her face and lifted her chin as she stared me down. But she was still Krista. Still a sweet, pretty girl who wanted nothing more than to be everyone's friend.

Wasn't she?

"I can't just take her. You know that," Steven Nell said, his watery eyes flicking over Krista like she was beneath his notice. "Rory Miller must come willingly."

He held his right arm around my middle like a vise, my back against his torso, and reached up to run his frigid, dry knuckles down my cheek. I could feel the random stubble on his chin pinching my skull through my hair as my head rubbed up against it. Bile rose up in the back of my throat. I squirmed, trying to wrench away from him, but he was strong. So much stronger than he'd been in life.

"Krista?" I said, pulse pounding furiously in my veins. Every inch of my body trembled, which pissed me off. I hated showing fear in front of Nell. "What the hell is going on?"

From the corner of my eye, I saw something shift in the darkness. A whisper of a figure. My father? Darcy? Could I still save them?

"I just want to go home," Krista said simply. "I don't belong here."

"That's what this is about?" I demanded. "You getting to go to your damn prom?"

"Don't you get it, Rory? I wasn't supposed to die," Krista snapped, bending at the waist. "You know it. I know it. And that night I brought Steven Nell up here, he told me the universe knew it, too. That it upsets the balance when someone takes their life by mistake. So he made me an offer. He wanted you for his eternal pet, but the Shadowlands won't just take a goody-goody Lifer like you unless you come willingly. And he knew how to make that happen."

"What about Darcy? She didn't come willingly," I said.

Krista smirked. "You forget: She wasn't a Lifer yet. Not officially."

"You're insane," I said, shaking my head, trying to pull away as Nell stroked my hair. "There's nothing that could make me sign up for an eternity with him."

"Oh, I think you will," Nell said lightly.

He lifted a lock of my hair and slowly drew it under his nose, sniffing it. A disgusting shudder of sheer pleasure rocked his entire body before he reverently touched it to his lips. My bottom lip wobbled and I closed my eyes, trying not to give Nell the satisfaction of hearing me sob.

"He gave me the tainted coins. He told me that if I ushered eighteen souls to the Shadowlands, including your little family"—Krista spat the word as if it had singed her tongue—"I could have what I wanted. I could have my life back. I got Pete to help me because I knew I couldn't overpower those people alone. Told him the Shadowlands would repay him for his hard work, too."

"What did you promise him?" I bit out.

"He wanted to see his brother again. Kid died when Pete was only eight years old. So I told him he could go to the Light and see him." Krista shrugged.

"And I'm guessing you never intended to deliver on that promise."

Krista smirked. "How could I? I'm just little old me. Little old *persuasive* me. It was just too bad Cori followed me, when I went to meet up with Pete that night after he 'disappeared,' and overheard us together. It really sucked, having to push her off that cliff."

My throat burned, and tears stung my eyes. I couldn't believe what I was hearing. Couldn't believe it was coming from Krista Parrish's mouth.

"Why eighteen souls?" I asked. "Why take my family?"

"Because he knew if I did that, he'd be able to cut another deal. With you."

I swallowed hard. My scalp tingled every time Nell's fingernails brushed my hair. "What?" I asked. "What deal?"

Krista took a step forward. Her eyes looked dead as she tilted her chin and got right in my face. "Your eternal soul for theirs."

My heart free-fell into my stomach. Nell started to laugh. I felt the breath of it against my ear. His scrawny body shook from the force of it, jarring against mine in fits and starts. I turned my head to gaze into the endless black. My family was in there somewhere, and I was the only one who could save them.

As long as I sacrificed myself.

Not that it was even a choice. Was there any way I could ever choose myself over them? They wouldn't even be dead if it weren't for me. If I hadn't gotten away from Nell that day in the woods, Darcy and Dad would still be alive. They'd be sad without me, sure, but they'd be alive and they'd move on. Instead, their lives were over and they'd just logged a few days in hell to boot, thanks to little old me.

The choice was clear. If it was either me suffering forever in the Shadowlands, or them, I picked me.

I looked down at my feet, a steely cold resolve coming over me. I knew they didn't deserve to be here, but in the end, in truth, didn't I? Nell might have been an evil bringer of death, but he was still a living human being, and I had killed him. I had done it on purpose. I had done it with malice in my heart. I had relished the act of it. In that moment, murdering him had felt good. It had felt right.

My dad and Darcy didn't belong in the Shadowlands. But maybe I did.

I closed my eyes and pictured my father, Darcy, my mom. In my mind's eye, I looked at each of them, solidifying their images in my mind, and said good-bye.

"No, Rory!" I heard Darcy scream, though whether it was

real or imagined, I had no idea. "No! Don't do it! Please!"

I blocked out her appeals, which made what I was about to do that much easier.

I opened my mouth to say it. To say yes, I would willingly go to the Shadowlands if the innocents would be set free. I looked up at Nell. His awful grin widened, deepening the lines on his face.

"I—"

"Rory, no!" Tristan's voice shouted. "Don't do it! It's a trap!"

A CHANCE

Tristan and Joaquin appeared out of the mist. Krista reeled around, yelling, and struck out at Joaquin. His eyes widened in surprise, but he reacted quickly. He grabbed her arm, pinned it to her side, and kicked her legs out from under her, shoving her face-first to the ground.

"What the hell is going on?" Joaquin asked me.

"She's the one who's been sending people to the Shadowlands," I said. "It was Krista the whole time."

Tristan and Joaquin exchanged a look, as if this didn't entirely surprise them.

"So Liam was telling the truth," Tristan said.

Joaquin knelt beside Krista, his lips a millimeter from her ear. "If I were you, I'd stay the hell down."

Then he shoved himself up and placed his foot on the small of her back.

"Rory." Tristan reached for me, but Nell pulled me back, a few steps farther into the abyss. I eyed Tristan desperately, wishing there was some way he could save me from this, like he'd saved me from so many other awful moments. But not even Tristan could fix this.

"Rory, listen to me. It was a setup," he said quickly. "Bea found Liam. It turns out he and Pete knew each other in the other world, and that was why they always acted so weird around each other. Liam didn't tell us, because he thought his connection to Pete might make us suspect him, and Pete didn't want to get Liam involved. But last night Krista let him go, hoping to distract us with another manhunt. He was with Lalani in her room by the docks, and he's fine."

"Okay. Okay, that's good," I said, trying as hard as I could to cling to something positive. At least Liam would be okay. Eventually. At least my first instincts about him had been correct.

"Pete's so-called confession was a setup," Tristan continued. "They wanted you to be alone—or sort of alone—when you heard it. Pete said Krista helped the Tse twins escape the mayor earlier and got them riled up again. The mob was just a distraction for the rest of us to deal with so she could get you to go into the jail alone and he could blurt it out to you—make you come up here. None of this is real."

"What about my family?" I said, glancing over my shoulder at the abyss. "They're real. And I can save them, Tristan."

"You don't know that." His voice was a high-pitched croak, his eyes rimmed with red. "We're talking about pure evil here, Rory. You really think you can trust anything he says? Anything they say?" he added, looking from Nell to Krista. "How do you know you don't say yes and then you're all just stuck here forever?"

The heavy reality of this possibility settled in over my shoulders.

"Are you calling me a liar?" Steven Nell asked, tightening his grip on me. Rage flared behind Tristan's eyes, and I could tell it was taking everything within him to keep from lashing out, to keep control. He didn't acknowledge Nell but looked directly at me.

"Don't do it, Rory. Please," he begged, inching toward me. "You don't deserve to spend eternity in the Shadowlands."

"Maybe I do. Maybe I don't," I told him. "And maybe this will work or maybe it won't. But, Tristan, I have to try. If there's a chance I can save my family, I have to try." I looked up at Nell, swallowing back my revulsion at the sight of his face, so very close to mine. "I'd like to say good-bye."

Nell's watery blue eyes softened as he looked at me, and somehow, that expression of caring was more horrifying than anything he'd ever done to me. It was as if he was calling me his with that one look.

"You have one minute," he said, releasing me.

I staggered away from him and threw myself at Tristan. He held me so close to his chest I couldn't separate his heartbeat from mine. I buried my face in his wet T-shirt, gasping for air.

"Don't," he said in my ear, his teeth clenched. "Don't you leave me. We're going to be together forever. Please, Rory. Don't do this. Don't."

I tilted my head up, and tears flowed freely down my face. "I'm so sorry, Tristan. I'm so sorry. I love you. I'll never stop loving you, I swear."

He leaned down and pressed his lips to mine firmly, desperately, longingly, and I kissed him back as hard as I could, trying to impress the memory of me into him, as if some piece of me could really linger there forever.

"I love you, too," he said.

"I know."

Somehow, I released him. I turned and looked at Joaquin. His chest was heaving, his eyes brimming with unshed tears. I stepped up to him, stood on my toes, touched his cheek, and kissed it.

"Good-bye."

He didn't say anything. He didn't have to. I knew how he felt. I knew what I was doing to both of them. But I also knew that I was doing the right thing. I stepped past Krista, who was smiling beneath Joaquin's boot, and stood in front of Nell.

"Don't," Tristan pleaded, tears streaming down his face. "Don't, don't, don't."

I lifted my chin, not letting myself consider what was to be.

"Yes," I said to Steven Nell, to my worst nightmare come to life. "I'll come with you."

"No!" Tristan screamed.

Steven Nell smiled. My ears, my head, my heart, my lungs filled with the awful sucking sound that meant it was over. That meant I was being swallowed whole. Devoured. Never to see my family, my home, my love again.

"Rory, no! Please, no!"

Tristan reached for me, his arm and hand and fingers stretching out in pure despair, and then he was gone.

THE CHOICE

"Rory. Rooreee! Time to wake up, sweetie. It's a whole new day."

I took a deep breath, clinging to sleep, knowing that if I opened my eyes, my mother's voice would cease to exist, just like she'd ceased to exist. She was singing my name, and I didn't want it to end.

"And I thought I was a heavy sleeper," Darcy said sarcastically.

"Give her a break." That was Dad. "She's been through a lot."

"Come on, sweetie." My mom gently shook my shoulder. "I want to look into your eyes."

I blinked myself awake. I was on a soft cotton pad on the floor of a vast white room, and I was staring at my mother's face. She looked nothing like she had on the day she died, with those sunken cheeks and milky eyes. She looked healthy. Perfect. Like she'd never been touched by cancer.

"Hey there. It's my baby," she said, her voice full.

I sat up and she enveloped me in a lilac-scented hug. Her blond hair brushed my face. I'd forgotten her hair, how long and soft it was.

"Mom? Where are we?" I looked up and saw my dad and Darcy standing behind her, wearing the same clothes they'd worn the nights they'd disappeared. Darcy in a tight blue T-shirt and jeans. Dad in his polo shirt and khakis. "I'm dreaming, right? This is a dream."

My mother reached out and tucked my hair behind my ears. "It's not a dream," she said, a proud smile lighting her face. "We're here because of you. We're together because of you."

"Me?"

"You committed a purely selfless act," my mother said, her hand coming to rest atop mine. It was so tan and perfect, her wedding ring shining on her ring finger. "You willingly gave yourself up to the Shadowlands to save those souls, and because of that, you were sent to the Light."

My heart leaped, and I looked at my father. "This is the Light? What about the others?"

"They're here," Darcy said with a smile. "Aaron is beside himself."

I laughed and tears overflowed, bathing my face. "And Nadia? Cori?"

"They've been here since they passed," my mom told me. "They were given the choice to return to Juniper Landing, but they chose to stay."

Relief hit my chest. "So I don't have to go to the Shadowlands? I don't have to be with—"

"Don't even say his name," my mother said, touching her fingertips to my lips. "You never need to say his name again."

I collapsed against her and cried, releasing the torrents of terror and confusion and uncertainty I had bottled up for so long. My mother hugged me close, her strength radiating through me. Just to be with her, just to be held by her again, was the greatest gift I could have ever been given.

"I'm so proud of you, sweetie," she said into my hair, kissing the top of my head. "Everything you've been through and everything you've done, and you're still my strong little girl."

"You've been watching me?" I asked through my tears.

"Of course. Are you kidding? I've been watching you since the moment I died," she said. She tipped my head back and held my face between her hands. "I never left you."

Then she looked at my dad and Darcy. "I never left any of you." She gazed into my eyes again. "And whatever you decide to do next, I'll always be right there beside you."

I felt a stab of foreboding. "Whatever I decide to do next?"

My mother nodded. She got up, tugging me by the hands to stand with her. We stepped off the cotton mat and onto the warm white floor. With one hand still clutching mine, my mother lifted the other and, palm out, wiped the air in front of us as if she were cleaning a window. Instantly, an image appeared. We were looking at the foot of the bridge, at Tristan, who was on his knees, and Joaquin, who stood over him. Tristan was sobbing, his shoulders bent, his hands flopped uselessly across his knees.

"What happened?" I asked. "Where's Krista?"

"Krista's deal was that she would be returned to Earth. Once your selfless act released those innocent souls, the Shadowlands drew her in for itself instead," my mother explained grimly. "As far as Tristan and Joaquin know, both of you are in the Shadowlands, and no one was ever released."

My mouth was dry as sand. "So they think I failed."

"They think you were tricked," my mother corrected. She took a breath and turned me to face her. "Now you need to decide whether you wish to stay here, in the Light, with us, or go back to Juniper Landing and continue your mission."

My heart thumped extra hard. I glanced over at my dad and Darcy. "What about you?" I asked my sister. "Do you get the same choice?"

"Yeah, but I already made it," she said. "I'm staying here."

"Oh."

"When I really thought about it, I realized I'm not gonna stay with Fisher forever, and if we break up, there's gonna be so much drama," Darcy said, rolling her eyes. "I'm sort of over all that, you know?"

"But what about being a Lifer? What about our mission?" I asked.

She lifted her shoulders. "I was never technically a Lifer. I never really got what it meant. Honestly . . . I think I'd rather stay here and just . . . be."

"Rory, we want you to know that whatever you decide, we're here for you and we're happy for you," my father said. "If you want to go back, we'll understand. And we'll always be with you."

I nodded, looking at my mom. The only thing I'd wanted for the past four years was to see her again. To hear her voice. To have her hug me and tell me everything was going to be okay. And there she was. Right there. Could I really imagine letting her go again?

"I want to be with you," I said plainly. "It's the only thing I've wanted since the second you told me you were sick."

"I know, sweetie."

"What's it like here?" I asked. "Are you happy?"

"I'm at peace," she said gently. "There's a certainty about being here. Knowing nothing can ever hurt you again. There's no confusion, no longing, no guilt. You just . . . are."

It sounded like perfection, never having to worry. Never feeling pain or uncertainty. But there was something leading in her tone. She was trying to tell me something. I looked her in the eye and flinched in understanding.

"But there's also no Tristan," I said. "No confusion, longing, pain, uncertainty, or guilt means no passion, too. No . . . love?"

"Oh, there's love," she said. "It's all around us. But it's not the same. It's not what you have with him."

She tilted her head and smiled. "C'mere," she said, holding out one hand.

I took it and she pulled me into her side, wrapping one arm around me and holding me close in a way that tickled me enough to make me laugh.

"You love him, don't you?" she said. "With all your heart?"

"Yeah," I croaked.

"And your mission there . . . it fulfilled you?" she asked. "It made you feel good, useful, accomplished?"

I straightened up, pulling away from her, and nodded, but my fingers still found her hand, unwilling to break apart for more than a second. "It did."

"I so looked forward to this when I was alive," she said, looking from me to Darcy. "That day you girls would come to me and tell me you'd found the one. And then, after everything that happened . . . " She looked away, then back to me, smiling. "The point is, I never thought I'd get to do it, yet here we are." She squeezed my hand, her eyes shimmering, and I knew she thought that I should go back. That I should be happy. That I should have a life, however odd and unconventional and of the unliving it was. "It's amazing how the universe works, isn't it?"

I nodded, a half sob, half laugh rumbling from my throat. "Yeah. It is."

"It's okay," my mother told me. She drew me into her chest and held me close, her chin against my shoulder. "It's okay, baby. You go. You be with him. You deserve to be happy."

"Mom," I choked out. "Mommy. I wish you could come with me."

"I know," she said. "I know. But we got through this once before. We can do it again." She pulled back and touched my face. "And who knows? Eternity is a long time. We may just find a way to meet up in the future. We Miller girls seem to have a way of getting around the rules."

I snorted a laugh, tears and snot running unbidden down my face—as if I cared. I turned around and hugged my dad good-bye. He was sturdy and strong for a good five seconds before he finally let out a ragged cry, and I nearly broke. Then I turned to Darcy, and she gripped me tight, her arms high around my shoulders as I clung to her skinny waist. She rubbed her hand in my hair and kissed my forehead.

"Tell Fisher I said good-bye," she told me. "And that other jerk, too."

I smiled. "Will do."

Then, finally, I returned to my mother for one last bolstering hug. She kissed one cheek, then the other, then my forehead, and put her hands on my shoulders.

"Never forget who you are," she said.

"Who is that again?" I asked tearfully.

"You're Rory Miller," she said. "You're strong and smart and fierce and defiant and compassionate and caring and true. You're my daughter, and I've got your back."

I smiled as best I could and tried not to choke as I said, "Thanks, Mom. For everything."

"You're welcome, baby."

For a long moment, we stood there, gazing at each other, and even though I knew this was good-bye, and even though my limbs felt heavy with sadness, this was so very different from the moment I'd said good-bye to her on Earth. There had been so much uncertainty then, so much finality, so much never-ever again. Now I knew where she was going to be, I knew she'd be safe, I knew she'd be watching. And the reality of that made my heart feel light.

My mom nodded, then turned me around slowly. Gradually, quietly, a vortex opened in front of us, this one white and long and far less intimidating. My mother leaned forward and whispered in my ear. "I love you."

"I love you, too," I said.

A velvet bag appeared in her hands, and she handed it to me. It was heavy, bulbous, and I had a feeling I knew what was inside. "Here," she said. "You're going to need these."

"Thanks, Mom," I said lightly. "You always did give the best presents."

She shrugged and kissed my forehead. "Your mom knows what you need better than anyone."

I smiled, turned around, and stepped through.

HOME AGAIN

When I returned to Juniper Landing, I was at the foot of the bridge, standing right behind Joaquin, who was standing right behind Tristan. It was as if no time had passed between the image my mom had shown me in the Light and this moment. Overhead, the clouds were starting to break up and disperse, giving way to small, jagged pieces of blue sky.

"Hey," I said. "Who died?"

Joaquin whirled around, so startled he almost lost his footing. "Rory?"

Tristan rose to his feet. He kept his back to me for what

felt like an eternity before finally turning around. His face looked haggard, like he hadn't slept in days. There were purple shadows under his eyes, and a tear clung to the underside of his chin.

"Too soon?" I asked, biting my bottom lip.

"Oh my god."

In two long strides, he closed the distance between us and pulled me into a deep, passionate kiss, his arms locking around me and bending me backward. As I held him, the heavy velvet bag my mom had given me rested against his back. I felt the warm sunlight against the side of my face and laughed even as I was kissing him.

Finally Tristan pulled away and looked into my eyes with wonder, brushing my hair back from my face. "I thought I'd lost you," he said. "I thought you were gone forever."

"I know," I said as the clouds continued to part. "So did I." I glanced at the deserted area around the bridge, the dozens of muddy footprints peppering the ground. "Where is everyone?"

"I sent them down to deal with the crowd," Tristan told me, holding on to my hand. "Hopefully they're getting things under control."

"What the hell happened in there?" Joaquin asked, hovering to my left. "Did Darcy and your dad get out?"

"Yeah. They're fine. Everyone's fine," I told them. "They

were released to the Light. Me, my dad, Darcy, Aaron, Jennifer . . . everyone. We ended up there." I cleared my throat. "Everyone except Krista."

There was a quick pulse of sadness, of dread. Until today, Krista had been one of our own, someone worthy of protecting, of loving. It was going to take a while for any of us to accept what she had tried to do.

A crackle split the silence. Bea's voice rang through our walkie-talkies. "Tristan? Are you there? Over."

He tugged his radio off his waistband and hit the button to talk. "I'm here. Everything okay? Over."

"Not exactly," she responded. "We managed to subdue part of the crowd, but the twins are on their way to you with about a dozen others, and they're not happy. Over."

"Damn," Joaquin said. "What're we gonna do?"

I felt the velvet bag hanging heavily from my wrist. "We'll use these."

I held the bag up, and Tristan's eyes widened. Joaquin leaned over and opened the knot cinching the top together. Dozens of gold coins glinted in the sunlight. Joaquin took the bag and held it with both hands.

"Where did you get these?" he asked.

I smiled, my eyes shining with tears. "From my mom."

"You saw your mom?" Tristan was stunned.

I took a deep breath. "Yeah. She gave me a choice: stay in the Light, or come back here and be with you guys."

In the distance, a truck engine roared. The visitors were coming. My heart thumped with trepidation, but I knew it would be okay. It might get a bit messy, but we would calm them, we would usher them, and they would go to the Light. Everything was going to be fine. For the first time in forever, I truly believed that.

Tristan held our hands up between us and kissed the backs of my fingers as he looked into my eyes.

"You could have been with your family," he said as he slowly processed the gravity of what I'd done. "But you chose to be here."

"I chose to be here," I replied, "because you are my family now. And this is where I belong."

The sun broke over his handsome face as he smiled and pulled me to him, holding me against his chest so I could feel the solidness of him, revel in the perfection of the moment.

We were together now—together in our world, together in our mission, together in our love—and nothing was ever going to tear us apart again.

Rory and Tristan.

Forever.

The first car appeared over the ridge, and Joaquin stepped up next to me, squaring off as if readying himself for a fight. I stood between him and Tristan and plucked a coin from the velvet bag with a small, determined smile.

"Boys." I flipped the coin and caught it as two car doors slammed and the twins marched toward us. "We have some work to do."

ACKNOWLEDGMENTS

As this bittersweet project comes to a close, I give huge and heartfelt thanks to the Lifers—

Lanie Davis
Emily Meehan
Sarah Burnes
Katie McGee
Logan Garrison
Laura Schreiber
Sara Shandler
Josh Bank

Les Morgenstein

Lizzy Mason

Jamie Baker

Kristin Marang

Liz Dresner

And my incredible fans, who are forever in my heart.